All Whom I Have Loved

All Whom I Have Loved

AHARON APPELFELD

Translated from the Hebrew by
ALOMA HALTER

SCHOCKEN BOOKS · NEW YORK

Translation copyright © 2007 by Schocken Books,
a division of Random House, Inc.

All rights reserved. Published in the United States by Schocken Books, a division of Random House, Inc., New York, and in Canada by Random House of Canada Limited, Toronto. Originally published in Israel as *Kol Asher Ahavti* by Keter Publishing House Ltd., Jerusalem, in 1999. Copyright © 1999 by Aharon Appelfeld.

Schocken Books and colophon are registered trademarks of Random House, Inc.

Library of Congress Cataloging-in-Publication Data
Appelfeld, Aron
[Kol asher ahavti. English]
All whom I have loved / Aharon Appelfeld;
translated from the Hebrew by Aloma Halter.
p.   cm.
ISBN 978-0-8052-4177-8
1. Holocaust, Jewish (1939–1945)—Ukraine—Fiction. 2. Jews—Europe, Eastern—Fiction. 3. Antisemitism—Soviet Union—Fiction. I. Halter, Aloma. II. Title.
PJ5054.A755K6513 2006
892.4′36—dc22   2006044283

www.schocken.com
Book design by Robert C. Olsson
Printed in the United States of America
First American Edition

2   4   6   8   9   7   5   3   1

All Whom I Have Loved

1

My father and my mother—their life together was not happy. They did not quarrel and they did not blame each other, but the silence in the house was as hard as ice and could have been sliced along its length. Sometimes my father's head would rise up, emerging out of this cold, as if he were about to shout. But this was just an illusion, for he did not raise his voice. I also learned not to disturb the silence, and I would sit on the floor playing dominos.

Father works until late, and when he appears at the front door, I put on my coat and go with him. We walk around the streets for hours and eventually we drop anchor in a café. Father drinks a coffee and I, a hot chocolate. People sit differently in a café than at home. They talk loudly and their voices flow. Only Father does not change. Sometimes it seems that among people his silence is more intense. In the evening he brings me back to my house. I still remember how he would sit on the floor and play dominos with me, go into the kitchen and prepare himself a cup of tea, and light a cigarette. Now he no longer crosses the threshold.

"Why doesn't Father come inside?" I ask Mother.

Mother shrugs and that's her answer. It's hard to know if she's hurt or angry. She, too, has learned how to keep silent. But in the evening, before I close my eyes, words return to her, and she sits on my bed and reads or tells me things. Her voice is open, her face full of light. The words flow from her, and it feels good to be close to her.

I turned nine, and Mother told me one day that Father would no longer be living with us but would come to visit me from time to time. I did not know what to ask and said nothing. Father is tall and lean, and even when he sits on the floor, he's taller than I am. With his legs crossed, he leans back on his arms. I knew that from then on we would no longer be playing at home, just in the park. In the park Father's silence is attentive; occasionally he'll say a word or a sentence, but aside from that, nothing.

On days when it's not raining, we walk along the river. Even here he hardly speaks. If I ask something, he'll answer with a word or two. On the way, we come across wooden houses with thatched roofs, wells from which sturdy peasant women pull up overflowing buckets, stray animals, and many wooden crosses, but most exciting of all are the chapels. They are usually near tall trees, and you can spot them by their miniature forms, as if children had built them. We go into one with our heads bent and are greeted by a small icon, at whose feet there's a shelf of dried flowers. There's a footstool on the floor, for kneeling. The icon is old and cracked, and the face of a tortured man gazes from it. In one of the chapels we see an icon of a young woman carrying a baby close to her bosom; wonder is diffused over her full features. Father loves chapels. Once he's inside, his face is all attention, and he's alert. Sometimes a light glows in the chapel, casting shadows on the icons.

The outing with Father lasts until dark. The darkness by the water is more frightening than the darkness near the trees, perhaps because it brings to mind a sleeping animal. I grip Father's large hand and overcome my fear.

When it's cold, Mother wraps me in a warm coat and a woolen hat and Father takes me downtown. In the center of town, the streets are wide and the chestnut trees throw their shadows on the sidewalk; at every corner there's a café or a fabric store. In the late afternoon a moist light hovers over the iron railings, and in the cafés a thick pall of cigarette smoke hangs in the air.

Father sits and plays chess with an elderly acquaintance. The man touches the chess piece and his hand trembles. When the game is most intense, I hear Father humming to himself. A game of chess can last an hour, sometimes two. Father plays and drinks coffee. I get a hot chocolate and a poppy seed cake. Father's fingers are long, his fingertips stained with tobacco. He moves the piece, dragging it slowly as if to say, that's it, no need to hurry, the enemy may be threatening, but he's not all that strong. It's easier for Father to talk to himself than to others. When he speaks to himself, entire sentences flow from his mouth. When he wins, he doesn't boast. With his back hunched over, he tries to appease his opponent.

It's already dark when we return home. The streets are empty, and here and there someone will pass, a lit cigarette in his mouth. When it's cold and there's a wind blowing, Father lifts me in his arms, and then I can see straight into the gardens and inside the windows of houses. Sometimes I see a girl sitting and playing the piano, and even though there is no one next to her, I imagine that someone is listening.

I want to ask Father many things, but I don't. I know that he doesn't like it when he's asked things, so I hold myself back and swallow the words. Sometimes we drop in at the tavern. Father downs a drink or two and we hurry to leave, yet I grasp how the tavern is different from a café. In the tavern, peasants sit around on the benches, heavy cigarettes hanging from their mouths. The air is dense with the smells of tobacco and beer, and young girls cheerfully pass around the tankards.

When I return home, Mother asks me: "How was it?"

To her question I respond with only "All right."

It's hard for me to part from what I've seen, and all through the night, these sights filter into my sleep. In sleep everything is different and sometimes the opposite, even Father's silence. Sometimes it seems that Father has lost control. His mouth is gaping open, and he is seized with fury, hitting people on both sides of him. People are scattering, but he's fast and grabs them; only when they promise to obey him does he let them go. I wake up from sheer terror. Mother rinses my face with water and takes me into her bed. It's hard to fall asleep again.

I see Father once a week. When he's away or busy, he doesn't come. His face disappears from my memory, and when he comes back, he seems like a different person.

2

Then it was summer, and Mother and I left for the country. The village is all woods and fields, and streams from the River Prut that winds through them. Mother rented a small house next to the water; she unpacked the suitcase and put on her green dressing gown. I stood at the window and saw no trace of streets, only children and sheep and horses galloping over the green fields.

Later, a peasant woman brought a basket with fruit, bread, and butter, and Mother paid her with two banknotes. The woman folded the notes, put them into a kerchief, and tied it up. Mother asked if she had vegetables in her garden, and the peasant woman smiled. "I have all kinds." She promised to bring some.

Then it was night, and Mother spread butter on slices of bread and served them on an earthenware plate. The bread was fresh and tasty, and with each bite I felt the tiredness from the journey. I tried very hard not to close my eyes, I drank water and I talked, but the tiredness was heavy and it overcame me. From within my sleep, I felt Mother's hands as she carried me to bed.

When I awoke, the sun was already full at the window. Mother prepared breakfast and said: "We'll soon go down to the river." We sat at the table, and we saw how the sun bathed the two rooms of the house with its light, and for a while we were filled with wonder.

This was how our vacation in the country began. We would get up early, eat something light, and then go to the river. The river was not deep and flowed quietly. The first dip would be cold, and immediately we would wrap ourselves in towels and jump around to warm up, but the higher the sun climbed, the more it would warm the water, and so we would dip in again and again. Mother would swim. Her strokes were rhythmic and supple. I was afraid when she swam out far and glad when she came back to me.

"Mother!" I'd call out with excitement.

"What?" she'd say, her arms reaching toward me.

I'd run and hug her legs.

Every few days we walked out farther, as far as the lake. The lake was in the heart of a forest, and its waters were black. Mother would dive and dive again, and at last she would take me in her arms and swim along with me. I would feel a fear full of pleasure, and we stayed in the heavy shadows for hours, bundled up in large towels, and only as the sun set would we pack the knapsack and return home. On the way back, we would sometimes come upon a calf or a colt. It would gaze at us for a moment and then flee, but apart from that, nothing stirred. The fields of clover had been harvested and appeared grayish, and the trees huddled together, ready for their nightly slumber.

In the afternoon the yard was shady, and Mother would spread out a reed mat, and we would sit and have tea. Mother baked a large cheesecake smothered with forest berries. We ate half of it and placed the rest in the pantry. Mother's dishes were so tasty that I ate and ate and asked for more.

At that time of the year the skies were aflame until late at night. Hues changed, and in the end what was left was a transparent gray with fragments of flickering fire. This thin grayness pressed us into the reed mat, and we gazed and gazed without tiring, but sometimes we got up to take a walk into the clear night and came back very late. And so we went on, day after day. The sun and the water enveloped us, and our skin became tanned. If it hadn't been for the nightmares that kept coming back to me, there would have been no pain at all there. Mother said that dreams don't tell the truth, but for some reason I did not believe her, even though it was plain to me that there were no monsters prowling in our backyard.

Sometimes the sun awakened me very early in the morning. Mother would still be sleeping, a sweet shadow hovering over her. I wanted to remove the shadow and gaze at her up close. It was hard to see her face, which would be wrapped in her long hair, but I could see her clothes, scattered on the chair and on the dresser. Mother's clothes were gauzy and satiny, pleasant to the touch, especially the silk stockings that she had bought just before our trip. I liked to watch how she stretched out her leg and drew the stocking up over it.

Sometimes, she woke up while I was gazing at her. "What are you doing, my love?" she'd ask.

"Nothing," I'd tell her, and I could not help laughing.

There, the days were long and went on deep into the night. Were it not for the few clouds, the difference between day and night would have been blurred. Sometimes a wagon full of children passed the house. The children would shout: "Jews! Jews!" and momentarily break the silence. But apart from these unexpected voices, there were no human sounds. The fields breathed quietly, and you could see the dark waves of night floating over the earth.

Sometimes fear gripped me, and I felt as if I was alone alongside the water. There was no reason for this fear. Whenever I called out "Mother!" her response was quick in coming: "I'm here!" Even when I awoke in terror and confusion, Mother leaned over to me and said out loud: "I'm here!" These magic words immediately took away the nightmare, and yet it would still be there when I closed my eyes.

"There are demons everywhere," said Mother.

"Here as well?"

"Even here, unfortunately."

"Can't you make them go away?"

"We'll drive them away," Mother promised.

I'd already heard the word "demons" in the city, and yet it was only there in the countryside that I understood at last what they looked like.

"The demons are small, aren't they?" I asked.

"True."

"And what do they do?"

"They pester people."

"That's all? Just pester?"

"On the whole."

Then it seemed to me that I'd seen them by the garden fence.

The days were clear, with not a cloud in the sky, and every day we returned to the river, to exactly the same place, as if we were trying to get to know it better and better. Mother had grown taller here; only I had stayed short. I was no longer afraid of the water, but I was still not ready to dip my head into it.

The time got shorter and shorter. Mother counted off the days on her fingers and said: "We have another week left." I found this counting unpleasant, and I wanted to say: "Mother, don't count like that," but I held back, so as not to make her sad.

But meanwhile we spent a lot of time at the lake. There, by the water, we were either naked or wrapped in large towels. There was not another soul inside this shadowy canopy. And yet I sensed we were in danger. "Mother," I'd call out, but Mother wasn't frightened. Alongside the brackish water she was lithe, her face open, and there was a moist sparkle in her eyes. She dove and surfaced, dove and uttered incomprehensible sentences. Once she put some squares of halva-covered chocolate on her palm and said, "Take it, my love, it's tasty."

"Mother, I'm not a bird," I said for some reason. When she heard this, Mother burst out laughing and hugged me.

Some Christian festival was being celebrated, and throughout the night cows and pigs were slaughtered in the village. The lowing and the squealing was enough to rend the heavens, but no one went to help them. I asked Mother if it was possible to save them, and Mother said it was their fate and that we couldn't change anything. The entire night I saw the blood flowing in the sky and pouring into the horizon.

The next day we didn't go to the river; Mother took me to the church. We walked along dirt roads and saw the clear morning like a canopy over the gardens. The fruit had already been picked from the trees, but on the highest branches a few large apples still swayed, reddish, as if drunken. At times we came upon a rooster or a sheep that would take fright at our footsteps; I was happy that they had been spared from the night slaughter.

"What do people do in the church?"

"Nothing. They pray."

"Will we pray, too?"

"No."

The church wasn't tall; it was domed, made of wooden beams, and a golden cross rose from the roof.

"Nice," said Mother, and we went inside.

The priest wore a long ceremonial robe and stood next to the altar. He read from a book, and the choir responded to him in song; there was a magnificence in this ceremony that deeply moved me. Mother must have been moved as well, for her face was tense and she grasped my hand. I was sorry that I had to be silent and didn't know how to sing the song that the choir and the worshippers were singing together.

After that, in a gesture that was slow and extremely impressive, the priest lifted a bowl of incense and waved it over the faces of those assembled. When they saw the smoke rising, they bowed their heads and I burst into tears.

"What's wrong, my love?" Mother bent down to me. "There's nothing to be afraid of."

I wasn't afraid; I was overwhelmed by the singing and the pungent incense.

The next day Mother packed our suitcase and paid the landlady. The landlady watched us with a kindly eye. "Where are you going?" she asked.

"Home," said Mother in a cold voice, and the openness in her face shut tight. I knew that if I were to ask her something, she would answer but in one word only. We still had two hours at our disposal, but Mother was in a hurry, as if the road beckoned to us.

3

It was night when our train arrived in Czernowitz. The station was in turmoil, with whistling trains and an overflow of people. We tried to make our way through, but all the exits were blocked. Seeing this reminded me of the nightmares that had kept me awake in the country. I gripped Mother's hand. Mother did not give up but tried again and again to push inside the waiting room with all her might. It was useless. People stronger than she shoved against us. In the end we were pushed aside, pressed against the wall.

We sat on the suitcase and waited for the crush to subside. I pictured the fields and the water that we had left behind, and longing choked me.

While we were sitting there hopelessly, Father appeared, as if the ground had split open and he'd emerged from it. He was wearing his usual clothes, but he looked so different here, as if he were a stranger. He immediately grasped the suitcase and led us outside through a dark opening. A carriage was waiting for us. Even now, Father behaved as he always did. He asked no questions. When we reached the house, he pulled down the suitcase, carried it up to the apartment, and said, "I'll come tomorrow." Then he was gone.

.   .   .

Mother had brought a few provisions from the country, and we sat down to eat. Her face was still tan from the country, but its freshness had faded. She tried to recall sights we had seen, but there was a hollow ring to her words.

Then, for no apparent reason, she began to cry. It was a bitter weeping that left her face blotchy. I fell at her feet, hugging her legs. Yet this time my love did not help. Her crying only intensified, as if drawing upon the depths of her hidden pain. I was so moved that when I went to bed I could not fall asleep. It then seemed to me that Mother was about to say, "I'm going to pack the suitcase, we're going back to the country. I feel out of place in this crowded city; everything is dirty and tasteless." But I was wrong; her sorrow passed and little by little she accepted our old place.

That same night Mother told me about her childhood. Her parents died young and she had grown up in an orphanage. The orphanage is at the edge of the town, near the trees and water. When she was nine, her class was taken to the city, and there she saw the Great Synagogue for the first time.

"And you didn't have any brothers or sisters?"

"No, I'm an only child," she said with a shy laugh.

At the age of twelve she was already an apprentice at the large garment workshop owned by the Stein family. She worked from morning till night, and in the evenings she studied. Eventually, she passed the matriculation examinations with low grades, but she graduated from the teachers' seminary with distinction.

"And do you remember your mother?"

"No. A few years ago, I could still remember some of

her features, but now they're gone. I remember that she was short."

"And was your father tall?"

"I don't remember. He died before my mother."

Mother opened her eyes very wide, so as to take in the distant visions, but it didn't help. To my questions she answered, "I don't remember; what I recall is so hazy."

I, at any rate, could imagine my mother's mother and father very clearly.

"I'm sorry, everything has faded from my memory," Mother said, shrugging.

"I will remember the house in the country and the water in the river. And the lake," I said for some reason.

"And me? Will you remember me, too?" she asked, suddenly putting me to the test.

"I'll remember you most of all." I wanted to impress her.

"How will you remember me?"

"Swimming in the water."

"Only swimming?"

"And wrapped in a large towel."

"What else?"

"And the song 'The Long Clear Nights of Summer'— the song you like to sing."

"I'm happy."

That night I slept soundly, but one clear image filtered into my sleep: Mother wearing a pure white nightdress.

4

Father came the next day and took me downtown. A month and a half in the country had effaced him from my memory. Father took long strides and I hopped along after him, getting tired. We stopped briefly, standing at a kiosk to drink some lemonade, and eventually we reached a café where Father loves to play chess. I find it hard to take his silence. It hurts me, and yet I still said, "Father," trying to be closer to him.

"What?" He opened his eyes, as if I'd stopped the flow of his thoughts.

Father played chess and I gazed at him. This time he opened his mouth and spoke, hummed, and leaned toward his opponent in a gesture of goodwill.

"Where have you been, child?" Father's elderly friend turned to me.

"In the country with Mother."

"And how was it there?"

"Good."

Father raised his head and smiled, happy that I revealed something to him that he would never have asked about.

"Paul knows his multiplication tables very well; you can test him," Father said.

"Seven times seven is what?"

I answered.

"I see that you're going to be even better than your father," said the elderly man without even looking at me.

We walked a lot that evening, and we also went to the tavern. Father's mood improved and he hummed a folk song, keeping time with his foot. Before I went into the house, he told me that the following week, when he got his salary, he would buy me a pair of high, laced boots.

The parting from Father was not hard, and yet it was not forgotten easily. The sight of his face did not leave me even when I sat next to the table and Mother gazed at me. Once, I said to my mother, "I love Father," and Mother's response was not slow in coming: "And don't you love me?" Since then I have chosen my words very carefully.

That night Mother told me that after I had left the house, a messenger delivered a letter to her with the news that she had been accepted as a teacher in a primary school in Storozynetz.

"Are we going there?"

"Of course."

Only later did I understand that this was not really about a journey so much as it was about being pulled away from everything I knew, and then a dark fear gripped me. That night my mother told me a lot about Storozynetz and about the beautiful fields that surround the small city. It was that night that I heard the phrase "garden city" for the first time, and it stuck in my head.

The next day Father came in the afternoon. The sun was still shining, and we went for a walk by the river. On the way we met a man dressed in black who was carrying a suitcase. The man turned to my father and asked him something. Father answered in a language that I did not understand. Then the man opened the suitcase and showed Father what he was selling, and Father chose two pencils and paid him. They talked, or, rather, the man talked, and he sounded as if he was complaining. Father, in his usual way, said only a word or two. For a moment the face of the man wrinkled up and it seemed that he was about to burst into tears. I was wrong: he burst out laughing, and Father did, too. His face opened momentarily as a smile emerged from his eyes. The man did not stop but continued talking, and Father laughed heartily.

"Who's the man?" I asked only when we had gone some distance from him.

"A Jewish peddler."

"What is a Jewish peddler?"

Father smiled as if I had embarrassed him, and said, "A peddler that belongs to the Jewish people."

"Is it a large people?"

"Not really."

"And everyone wears black?"

"No."

Then we went into a tavern. Father gulped down a small shot glass, flirted with the waitress, and complimented her. The waitress did not blush. It was obvious she was used to compliments. After the tavern we went straight home, and Father uttered not a word the entire way.

5

Mother is packing feverishly. It's hard to know if she's happy. The apartment is very small, but it has a window that faces the park. In the afternoons, elderly people from the old-age home sit in the park. I stand at the window and gaze at them, and the more I gaze at them, the more I feel that their thoughts touch my thoughts.

Father doesn't come. I wait for him every afternoon. He is sick and is away. His absence, like his silence, pains me, and for tense hours I wait for him.

Mother stuffs utensils and clothes into the suitcases. The two suitcases are already full, and yet still she crams more into them. Her movements are full of force and bring to mind a destructive anger.

Later, a driver comes and loads the suitcases onto a wagon, then we climb up as well. It's the first time that I've ridden in a simple open wagon in the city. I feel as though everyone is looking at me. Mother, too, seems embarrassed, for she wears a broad-brimmed hat and sunglasses.

At the station, porters help us, taking the suitcases and the bags to the train. The porters are so tall and so broad that they seem like a different breed of people. Mother pays them, but they demand more, and Mother gives in to them without bargaining.

We sit in the second-class car and Mother's face is restored to her. She tells me that in the garden city we will have a large house with a porch and a garden. When Mother is comfortable she likes to describe things, and I can picture them vividly. Sometimes the place or the person doesn't bear any resemblance to what she has described, perhaps because when she gets enthusiastic she exaggerates. I love her exaggerations — they suit her.

The journey passes quietly. Though there are some drunks in the car, there are no fights. We eat sandwiches and drink lemonade, and we gaze at the passing landscape. At one of the stations we get off and Mother buys me an ice-cream cone. It is pink and tasty and reminds me of another ice cream that I ate with Father in a remote place next to an old chapel.

Then I fall asleep, and in my sleep I see black peddlers like the ones I saw at the riverbank. They are huddled together next to a tall tree. When they discover me, they turn toward me and ask how Father is. I freeze in fear. I want to run away but my legs are tied.

I awake in fright and confusion. Mother kisses my forehead and rubs my shoulders to take away my bad dream. Whenever I have bad dreams, Mother says, "Every sleep has bad dreams. It's only a deception." But what's to be done? The dreams awaken me even when they disappear. Sometimes they cling to me the entire day, returning at night, and sometimes I have a bad dream that goes on for an entire week.

While the train hurtles on, a man approaches Mother and addresses her by name. It turns out that he is an old acquaintance. He and Mother studied together at the teachers' seminary, and they haven't seen each other for years. He immediately joins us and they become immersed in a lighthearted conversation. Mother knows how to make people happy, but her openness actually makes me sad. When she tells stories and gets enthusiastic she forgets me, and I feel neglected. Once, she met a friend from the orphanage, and she was so happy that she left me on a bench in the park. "Mother!" I shouted, but she didn't hear me. People gathered around me, asked my name, and offered me candies. I was in despair, and I shouted, "Mother! Mother!" Eventually she came back and collected me.

Now the strange man sits and chats with Mother; they laugh and recall lighthearted memories. I stare at the man's face and I can't find a single pleasing feature in it. He's shorter than Mother, bald, and he wears glasses. Apparently Mother doesn't see the defects that I see; she listens to him and they recall names and places that sound strange and unpleasant to me. It's hard for me to take this lightheartedness, and I want to shout, "Stop this chattering, it hurts me!" But of course I hold it in and don't say a word.

Eventually, I feel sick and I throw up. Mother hastens to my side and holds my forehead.

The train has stopped. We get off, and Mother rinses out my mouth with water. The stranger parts from Mother, wishing her good luck in her new position. The train goes on its way, and I'm glad that there is no longer anyone between me and my mother. I cry, and Mother, who does not understand my tears, says, "What's come over you? Does something hurt you?"

She doesn't know that I am crying from sheer happiness.

6

This time Mother has not exaggerated. The new house is large, and behind it a garden stretches all the way to the forest. "I told you," Mother says, and there is a mischievous sparkle in her eyes. She will soon begin teaching, but in the meantime there is plenty of time for us to go on walks and outings. Although a small town, Storozynetz does have some splendid stores and a café. Behind the houses and the stores, the fields and the orchards go on and on, and the farther we get from the town, the more I feel my life expanding. It is good to be near Mother.

"Mother," I say, and she holds my hand tightly.

In the afternoon we sit on the mat behind the house. The landlord comes by to ask if everything is all right and if we need anything. He's short and he speaks German with a heavy accent, but he has a kind face and it seems that we won't have any differences of opinion, as we did with the landlord in Czernowitz.

In the evening Mother lights the large oil lamp and the dusky kitchen fills with light. We eat only vegetables, fruit, and dairy products and do not touch meat. One mustn't kill animals, Mother once said. I'm afraid to look the cows in the pasture in the eye. They seem to know what their fate is and are asking me to save them.

Dinner lasts about an hour. In Czernowitz, Mother gave private lessons, with students arriving one after another and filling our small apartment with unquiet. At night, Mother would complain of headaches and would lie in bed with a damp cloth on her forehead. Now she doesn't complain. Her headaches seem to have stopped.

After dinner we sit in the bedroom, and Mother reads me *Alice's Adventures in Wonderland*. I'm so excited that Mother is near me that I find it hard to fall asleep. Even when I'm in bed, we go on talking. Mother reminisces about our vacation in the country, and suddenly all the images I stored up come to life. The river there wasn't deep or swiftly flowing, and perhaps this is why I remember it so well. I'm afraid that these clear images will be erased from my memory, and I repeat to myself: they won't be wiped away, they won't disappear, they will always be with me just as Mother will always be with me. But this very repetition stirs in me a deep sorrow that insinuates itself within me and resurfaces the next evening at twilight, when we come back from the street and stand in front of the house.

"Mother," I say.

"What is it, my love?"

"Will we return to that village?"

"Why are you asking, my love?"

"I'm afraid that the village will disappear."

"It won't disappear," Mother says, and opens the door.

Even as our days are rich and overflowing, I discover that next door to us is a low structure, quite simple, surrounded by a fence, its yard full of bearded men.

"Who are they?"

"Jews."

"What are they doing here?"

"They've come to pray."

The bearded Jews frighten me, and when I stare at them from up close, they seem to be hiding something. Their movements are hasty and they're talking in whispers. I tell Mother what I'm thinking and she laughs, saying, "They're just like anyone else."

Their prayer is also strange, a mixture of calls and shouts.

"That's the way they pray," Mother says.

"Why are they shouting?"

"So that God will hear them."

Meanwhile, we spend most of the day outside. We eat lunch in a restaurant, dressed in warm clothes. Sometimes it seems to me that we're only on vacation here, and that we'll soon return to Czernowitz. Sometimes, a man who looks exactly like my father passes us. I let go of Mother's hand and run toward him, but I realize immediately that I am mistaken. And when the evening is clear and there's no rain, we walk all the way down the main street and then on toward the fields. The fields are flat and open, and even if we walked the entire night, we would not reach the horizon.

7

As we became ever more enchanted with provincial life, Father appeared. He stood in the doorway, dressed in a gray suit, and I hardly recognized his swarthy face.

"Father!" I called.

His face lit up a bit.

Mother offered him a cup of coffee, but Father refused, saying: "I've come to see Paul; I'll bring him back by evening."

It was strange: I had almost forgotten him.

"And how is it here?" he asked when we were out of the house.

"It's good."

We crossed the main street and strolled around the alleyways. Eventually we went into the café where I had sat with Mother. The cloud seemed to lift from Father's face, and I saw that he was squinting, as if he were unused to the light.

I couldn't bear his silence, and I asked: "How was the journey here, Father?"

"Splendid," he answered, and it was obvious that he wanted to make me happy.

.   .   .

One evening Mother revealed to me that Father had been a painter and was successful when he was young, but that later on he had stopped painting. Now, for a living, he taught art at a high school. He didn't enjoy his profession, and most of the time he was very depressed.

"What's depression?" I fumbled like a blind person. Mother explained this word in different ways, but her explanations clarified nothing for me. Much later I envisioned Father pressed between two iron boards and felt a pain in my chest.

I sat in the café with Father. He drank a cup of coffee and smoked a cigarette. It was hard for me to imagine Father without a cigarette; sometimes it stayed stuck to his lower lip. "In another week the school year starts," he said, and I felt that this burden weighed heavily upon him. I tried to picture him sitting and painting. It was easier to imagine him looking at a painting than painting. When he looked at a painting he had a sour expression, as if there were a serious defect in it.

Father sat next to me and didn't speak. In my imagination, I recalled the places he'd taken me. The chapels, of course. He was extremely fond of these little shrines where passersby stopped to pray. Once, he said to me: "The icons in the chapels are so beautiful, it's only natural that they be used by those who worship God."

Mother also told me that in recent years Father had become addicted to drink, and that he squandered most of his salary on it. It was hard for me to picture Father staggering and cursing in the streets like the drunks whom we came upon every Saturday evening.

When we left the café, we walked all the way down the main street again. It was clear that Father did not like the provinces. I tried to pull him toward the fields, but he refused, shrugging. We wandered around the houses and the stores. Finally we went into a tavern. Father gulped down two shot glasses and said, "That's more like it."

When we arrived home, Father kissed me on my forehead but did not come into the house. He seemed a little more stooped, and his long arms hung limply. I wanted to call out, "Father, when will we meet again?" But I didn't manage to—he was already far off.

I watched how he walked. At first he walked in the middle of the street and kept turning his head to the side, and the farther he went, the clearer it was to me that he was looking for shelter from the harsh light in the street. Finally, he turned onto a dark side street and disappeared.

When I came in, Mother asked, "How was it?"

"We walked around," I answered.

Only later did I feel the touch of Father's fingers, as if he were still holding my hand. I tried to remember what he had said to me, but I could recall nothing. His unmoving eyes continued to gaze at me for a long time.

Mother was making posters for her classes for the coming school year. I was glad that she left me alone and did not ask anything more. Each meeting with Father left me mute, as if he had poured his silence into me. Sometimes it seems to me that I'm like him, but when Mother holds out her hand to me, her mouth open and her eyes laughing, I immediately meld into her joyfulness.

8

I dreamed a dream, and in my dream I saw Father becoming more and more distant from me. He was taller than his usual height, and he towered like a giant over everyone in the street. People stared at him, as if he were some marvel that had sprung up before their very eyes. I stood at a distance and also marveled, but as he came nearer, Father seemed to shrink more and more, and people ceased paying attention to him, and eventually he disappeared into the darkness.

Shocked and frightened, I awoke. I remembered the dream clearly and I told it to Mother. Mother hugged me and said, "It's a dream, it'll pass." And she closed her eyes. I felt a distance in her words, perhaps because she hadn't heard me out. I gazed at her sleeping face, and I was astonished that she didn't sense that I was awake. "Mother," I called, but she didn't answer.

And so the night passed. The next day, a slim young Ruthenian girl came to us, and Mother said, "This is Halina. Halina will look after you and play with you. I'm starting to teach."

Mother showed Halina the kitchen and the bedroom and said, "Paul loves to take walks. Take him for walks in the streets and in the fields." Then she picked up her briefcase, kissed me on my forehead, and left. I was in shock, and I didn't see her go out.

My mother tongue was German, and Halina spoke Ruthenian. She knew a few words of German and laughingly ticked them off on her fingers.

I stared at her, and it seemed that this was still the dream from the night before, that I was alone in the world among strangers, and that the person who had been brought to take care of me spoke a language that I didn't understand. "Get out of here," I wanted to shout, but I choked and burst into tears. Halina tried to calm me. She cavorted and jumped up and down, she imitated birds and frogs, but the tears that were stored in me grew stronger and stronger. To distract me, she knelt down and wept with me, but even this ruse did not calm me.

I stood there and wept, and the tears seemed to flow back into me. Eventually I grew tired and fell asleep on the floor. When I awoke and saw Halina, I let out a shout. Halina must have been frightened, because she took me outside. "Take me to Mother! I want my mother!" I yelled, drumming my legs on the ground. Unfamiliar neighbors gathered around and tried to calm me, but I was so immersed in my tears that their every word only stoked my rage. Eventually they said to Halina: "There's no choice, take him to his mother, take him to the school."

I wailed all the way to the school. Everything was a blur, but I did see the two-story building and the yard full of noisy children. My crying amused them, and they made fun of me. Halina scolded them and pulled me toward the teachers' room.

Mother saw me and was shocked. In her panic she let out a cry that sounded like she was choking. I was completely overcome with weeping and anger, and I lay on the floor, kicking my legs. Mother knelt and said, "I'm here, my love." The words barely penetrated my ears. Finally I got to my feet and dragged her outside. Mother didn't resist but let herself be dragged along behind me. I saw she was clenching her jaw, but she didn't rebuke me. The entire way home she tried to distract me by saying things to me, and at the kiosk she bought me an ice cream. Halina stood as if she had been reprimanded, ready to do as she was told. Mother asked her something in her language, and Halina shrugged and said, "What could I do?"

Halina went on her way, and Mother and I entered the house. Mother sat by the table and said nothing of my behavior. I felt that she was waiting for me to come to her and apologize, but something in me refused to do this. Mother went to prepare lunch and I sat on the floor. Suddenly I heard her say, "You'll have to get used to it." *To get used to it* — I'd already heard this cold expression, but this time it sounded like ice falling from the roof in the winter.

"Mother."

"What?"

"When is Father coming back?"

"I don't know."

We ate dinner in silence. A wall of silence had suddenly sprung up between Mother and me. Toward the end of the meal, Mother tried to placate me, but I felt that her words came from her lips and not from her heart. Before going to sleep she said, "I have to go to work. I have no choice. You're a big boy and you understand."

When I didn't respond she began to cry. In the city she would sometimes cry over Father's behavior, about his wastefulness and the times he didn't come home. But this was a different kind of weeping; it was sharper and more bitter, as if she were saying, "You, too? You're ganging up with your father so as to hurt me?"

I didn't know what to do, and I knelt down.

"Don't make it so hard for me," she implored.

"I won't make it hard."

"I'm a new teacher and everyone's watching me."

"I won't cry, I promise."

Mother dried her eyes. Her face, which had become swollen from her tears, returned to itself, and she said, "What can I do? I have to go out to work. There's no one to support us."

Her words sounded rehearsed, but the more she said, the clearer it became that I would not be able to stop the nanny from coming the next day. So as not to show how much it hurt me and to please her, I said, "Don't worry about it, Mother. I'll go to the park with Halina."

9

The next day I stood by the door and said good-bye to Mother. I did not cry. I felt the anguish of parting later, in the bedroom, amidst the rumpled bed and scattered clothes. It was a sunny day, and the yard behind the house was filled with light. We went out, and Halina immediately began to show me her wonders: she walked on her hands and then made noises like the cawing of crows; she imitated sheep and cows, frogs and cuckoos. And for a moment she seemed to be not a person but an amazing animal that knew how to do everything that animals can do: to climb trees nimbly, to crawl, to leap over fences, and to fly. Halina lost no time in trying to teach me her skills, but I was far from agile and scarcely capable of producing a single whistle.

Then we rolled in the grass. Halina was slender and very nimble. I tried hard to catch her, but she ran fast and could hop like a rabbit. I stared at her and I knew: I would never be able to do the same.

And so the day passed. The pain of parting from Mother had pierced through me, but Halina was so entertaining that as the time passed I no longer felt it. When Mother returned home, I was playing marbles with Halina and I didn't hear her footsteps. She came in, immediately threw her briefcase onto the floor, and sat down on the sofa. As she stretched out and leaned back, she said, "How was it?"

"We played."

"You didn't take a walk?"

"We took a walk."

The following day Halina repeated her tricks. We had a mid-morning snack, then we left for a walk along the main street, and from there we went down to the market. Now I saw the Ruthenian peasant women up close. They had spread out their vegetables and fruits on sacking and on low stalls. Some of their fowl were trussed up, and most were in cages. I saw them and it pained me.

And so the morning passed. Halina would point to something and ask me its name in German. She found it hard to pronounce the words that I taught her. Everything amused her and she laughed. I found it hard to laugh, even when I was rolling in the grass.

Mother came back from the school tired, her face as pale as chalk. She told me about the children who came from the villages, who found it hard to learn and were disruptive. The vestiges of anger could still be seen in her face, and for a moment she closed her eyes and rested her head on the back of the chair.

We ate a late lunch on the porch. At this time of day, the porch was still filled with light. I wanted to make Mother happy, but I wasn't sure how. I told her that I was at the market but didn't tell her about the trussed chickens so as not to make her sad.

In the afternoon we stayed in the house. Mother lay on the bed, a cloth to her forehead. The headaches that she used to get in the city had now returned, with greater ferocity. She lay without uttering a sound.

When the light dimmed I went outside and approached the yard that faced our backyard, where the bearded Jews would gather. Up close, I saw that they were not only different in the way they dressed but in their movements, too. They seemed to have a secret, and to move this secret from hiding place to hiding place. When the secret was well hidden they went inside to pray. Their prayer was noisy and sometimes they shouted. It didn't go on for long, and afterward they gathered again in the yard. Darkness fell and blackened their faces. I very much wanted to go in there and touch their secret, but I was afraid. I feared that if they touched me, I would get a rash, like the one I'd had in the winter.

I went back and asked Mother about the bearded Jews, and she explained to me that they were old Jews, and that their way of life was different from ours. It was hard for me to really understand her and yet I did pick up some of what she'd said. Mother was so occupied with things at school that her heart, I felt, was no longer with me. She was up till late at night, correcting exercise books and preparing posters. Sometimes she fell asleep in her clothes, without putting out the light.

Finally, I summoned up the courage to go into the yard of the bearded Jews. Surprised, they gathered around me and asked what my name was and where I lived. I told them my name and pointed to the house.

"You live right next to us," they said in amazement. One of them took a piece of candy out of his coat pocket and gave it to me. From up close, they were not so short. They spoke a jumbled language, with a strange pronunciation, and they swallowed their words. But I still understood some of what they were saying.

"Where are you from?" one of them asked.

I told him.

"And how long will you live here?"

"Always."

When they heard this, they were amused, as if I had told them something funny. "And what are you doing?" I asked, and was immediately taken aback by my own question.

"We are praying. Do you want to pray?"

"I don't know how."

They stared at me and I stared back at them. Eventually one of them said to me, "Go back home, child, your mother must be worried."

I went back to the fence, bent down, and put a leg over the post. I was in our yard. It was so different from theirs, it was as if I had returned from another city.

I told Mother about the visit. She lifted her head up from the notebooks and did not scold me.

"Are they Jews?" I asked, even though she had told me that they were.

"That's right."

"And what's the difference between the old Jews and the new Jews?"

"The old Jews believe in God and pray to him."

"And new Jews don't believe in God?"

"No."

Usually when Mother explained something she would go into detail, but this time she made do with one word and then buried her head in the pile of notebooks. Ever since she'd started teaching she'd become tired and distracted, and I felt that her enthusiasm had been dampened. But she kept repeating that one can't be tough with the village children, for their lives were harder than ours.

10

Yesterday Mother turned twenty-nine, and the two of us celebrated her birthday on the porch, at the round table that was covered with a white tablecloth. Mother was in high spirits; she lifted a glass of wine and made a toast: "To living!"

When Mother is filled with enthusiasm, her beauty shines out, and I feel sad that she has to spend most of the day in school with the unruly peasant children and about the headaches that don't leave her alone. To make her happy, I told her about Halina's feats: how she skipped, and how she imitated things. Mother listened but said nothing, and for a moment it seemed that my words did not touch her. It was a mistake, of course. What I said made her glad, for she immediately promised me that during Christmas vacation we would travel to the Carpathian Mountains.

"Are there rivers in the Carpathians?" I asked.

"There certainly are, but in the winter they're frozen over."

"And what will we do there?"

"We'll ski."

The word "ski" had such a wonderful sound that I immediately pictured the high hills, and Mother and I in winter coats, borne along on gusts of wind and floating over the surface of the white snow.

After the meal we went for a walk. It was a pleasant evening, wet from the afternoon rains, and we took the dirt track to the fields. At this time of the year the fields were gray and sad, and a kind of dull lowing rose from the dark valleys. Suddenly Mother went back to talking about the crowded classes at the school, the noise, and the uproar in the corridors.

We made our way back along the avenue of chestnut trees that led from the fields to the city. The trees were already bare, and their large leaves lay on the ground yellow and trampled. The farther we went, the more the damp evening seemed to bring to mind other evenings, but where and when I do not know. Since we'd left Father in Czernowitz, it was as if my life had been torn in two. Sometimes it seemed that I was walking with him and breathing in his silence and the scent of his cigarettes.

Suddenly the lights of evening turned red, and I saw Father standing next to me, and it wasn't only him I saw but the street that leads to the tavern as well. But then people were addressing him, and he wasn't answering. Speech was frozen in him, and only when the waitress had served him his third drink did a thin crack of a smile spread across his face, and he called out: "To all those who sit in taverns, and to all those wretched people who have never tasted a drink." On hearing this, the waitress burst out laughing and said, "Where did you get that toast from?"

"From the heart."

For a moment I was very indignant that on Mother's birthday my thoughts were with Father. "Mother," I said, wanting to apologize.

"What, my love?" Mother asked tenderly.

"I love you so much."

"Me, too," she said, and kissed my head.

When we returned home, Mother got another one of her headaches. She lay on the bed and I sat next to her. When she had these headaches, I wouldn't speak to her. I gazed at her breathing and at her hair gathered behind her. For a long time I sat and gazed at her, and eventually I fell asleep.

The next day Halina came wearing an embroidered linen dress. She had already learned some words of German and I some words of Ruthenian, but it was hard for us to speak. I told her about Mother's birthday and about the evening walk along the avenue of chestnut trees. The story did not impress her. Her thoughts were usually on birds; they were not afraid of her, and they would come to peck seeds from her palms. She would stroke them and speak to them, and put them on her shoulders. They were in no hurry to fly away.

"Halina, what language do you speak to them?"

"Ruthenian."

"And they understand?"

"Every word," she said, and burst out laughing.

Her eyes and hands were more fluent than her mouth. With her hands, she explained many things to me. Her gestures no longer seemed strange. I noticed that around her neck she wore a chain with Jesus on the cross. I had seen the crucified Jesus Christ on my walks with Father when we visited the chapels. I asked Father a lot about him and his crucifixion. Father's explanations were so abrupt that it was hard to understand them.

"What's this?" I asked Halina, and I pointed to the cross.

She raised her hand and with a finger pointed to the sky.

"He's God? Really?"

It was hard for me to understand how God, who's so mighty, could squeeze himself down into a simple likeness, so He could be worn around someone's neck. I wanted to ask her about this, but I didn't know how.

Later Halina surprised me and asked, "How old are you?"

I told her.

"And why don't you go to school?"

"I have asthma."

"What is asthma?"

I told her.

"You poor thing."

I'm not a poor thing, I was about to say.

"How many years have you had the illness?" she asked.

"From childhood."

"And are you suffering right now?"

"Now I'm breathing like a bird." I tried to impress her.

My mysterious illness was a secret between Father and myself. In my early childhood, a doctor diagnosed asthma. Father latched on to this and had me exempted from school. Apparently Mother was against this, but Father returned triumphant from the Ministry of Education: "I've got Paul exempted from the house of slavery."

I was then six years old. Many events have been erased from my memory, but not the sight of Father on his return from the Ministry of Education. For he had freed me not only from school but from all the hardships that awaited me in life.

11

Even as autumn darkens the windows of the house, Mother tells me that from now on she will also be working in the afternoons, and Halina will look after me all day. I do not ask why. Halina is pleasant company; we play hide-and-seek and entice birds to us with crumbs of bread, we play on the main street and in the fields, and when it's not raining we go to the river. By the time Mother returns at night, I'm so immersed in our games that I scarcely notice her.

Halina tells Mother what we've done and what I've eaten. In the afternoon she bathes me in a large tub, puts me on her knees to dry me, and declares, "Such a nice strong boy, all the girls will want to kiss him!" Then she sinks her mouth into my upper arms and my thighs and adds, "Very tasty, the tastiest."

This hurts a little but it is not without pleasure. She dresses me in a sailor outfit.

Every day Halina learns new words and immediately uses them; I learn, too, but not as fast. Sometimes we sit on the banks of the river and talk. Halina lives in a village near Storozynetz, and she has a fiancé. The fiancé is in the army, and she plans to marry him when he is released.

"Is he handsome?" I ask.

"Yes, he's handsome," she says, and for some reason it hurts me.

"When does he come?" I ask her.

"From time to time."

That is a slight consolation. I feel that I have already known Halina for a long time—since my walk with Father along the banks of the Prut, when I saw the girls doing their washing on its banks, except that then she was distant and unattainable and now she is so near me, I can touch her neck.

Mother has changed over the past weeks: she still complains about headaches, but less frequently. Now a hidden smile plays on her lips. She sits and corrects notebooks late into the night.

"What's happened, Mother?" I have to ask.

"Nothing, why?"

At first glance, there's no change at all, but when she gets up and goes to the writing table, I notice a movement I haven't seen before. She pulls back her hair with both her hands, shakes her head, and then lets it fall loose. Mother has long, golden tresses, which used to be gathered in a heavy braid. When we left the city and moved to the provinces, she cut off the braid, but her hair is still long and flowing and looks lovely on her back.

We sleep together in a wide bed. I usually sleep deeply now and seldom awaken at night, but sometimes toward morning I awaken and gaze at Mother's face. I see that she is fighting off bad dreams, and I want to wake her up and help free her from the clutches of the demons. But in recent weeks, I've noticed that her sleep is calm and her lips parted, and she seems to be smiling.

"Mother, you were smiling in your sleep," I tell her.

"Was I?"

"I saw you smile."

"Perhaps."

The rain falls incessantly. Halina no longer takes me out to the fields, and most of the day we sit on the floor or by the window. When the rain lets up, we go to buy ice cream. At the end of the street, Halina has found a shack where they sell homemade ice cream. It's soft and tasty. Then we hurry back home so that we won't be caught in a sudden shower.

In the afternoon, the windows darken even more. Halina sits and knits and I sit and daydream. My daydreams are sometimes so real that they make me dizzy. "Halina!" I shout. Immediately she comes to me and enfolds me in her arms, explaining that bad thoughts are the waste products of good thoughts and that they have to be cleansed from one's mind.

"How do you cleanse the mind?"

"With song."

So she begins to sing, and I fall asleep in her lap. I sleep for an hour, sometimes two. This sleep in Halina's lap is a soft sleep. She strokes my head and sings quietly. Sometimes I sleep until Mother returns.

When Mother comes into the house, Halina says, "The child is sleeping." I hear her voice clearly but don't open my eyes. Halina tells Mother everything she's done and everything that we've done together. She concludes by saying, "The child's already been sleeping for two hours."

Now I expect Mother to come over to me, but she doesn't. She takes off her clothes, puts on her dressing gown, and sits in front of the mirror for a long time, cleaning her face. I'm upset that she doesn't come to me and doesn't ask how I am. I've already noticed that in recent weeks she makes up her face frequently, she is easily confused, and in the morning she leaves but immediately returns—she's forgotten the key to her classroom or her umbrella. I have no doubt that there's something going on with her; all her movements tell me. Sometimes she seems angry with me for watching her so carefully. I'm afraid of my thoughts and tell myself over and over again that Mother would never abandon me.

Halina again surprises me. "Don't you want to go to school?"

"No."

"All Jewish children excel at their studies—don't you want to be outstanding?"

"No."

"Strange."

Mother had tried a few times to have the ban that Father had put on my schooling rescinded, but Father stood his ground and it never happened. Sometimes I believe that Father invented my sickness only to free me from school. Father hates schools and vowed, in his heart of hearts, that he would never send me to one.

"Who taught you how to learn by yourself?" Halina asks.

"Father. You can test me," I say, sure of myself.

"Me?" Halina bursts out laughing. "I should test you? I've forgotten everything I learned."

12

Just as autumn was bearing down and it began to rain incessantly, Father appeared. He was probably surprised to find Halina at home, since he said, "I'm Paul's father." Halina moved aside and blushed. I was also astonished, but I immediately recovered and ran toward him.

During the preceding weeks, I hadn't thought about him. He would appear to me sometimes in dreams but as a fleeting shadow. Now he stood there, as if he had come from a different world. I almost said, "Where have you come from, Father?" Halina says that you should not reveal all your thoughts, and so I didn't this time.

A fine rain was falling, and Father covered the two of us with his large umbrella as we left the house. He seemed to have grown taller since I had last seen him. I must have been wrong. We walked down the main street, with Father striding along on my right. His silence was unchanged, and I comforted myself by thinking that we'd soon be sitting in a café. In a café he sometimes came out with some complete, understandable sentences. This time he surprised me; we went straight to a tavern. There was a statue of a black horse at the entrance.

It was three o'clock and the bar was almost empty. Father had brought me a gift: a wristwatch. He immediately put it on my left wrist. I was so moved that tears pricked my eyes. I had known how to tell time from the age of five. Mother was proud of my knowledge in math, and whenever we were sitting around the table or taking a walk, she would give me an exercise and I would work it out.

Father must have forgotten that I knew how to tell time. When I accurately did so, he gulped down his drink with joy and laughter. When Father has a bit too much to drink, his closed face opens up slightly. I told him I also knew fractions. He immediately gave me an exercise, and I solved it easily. "A head full of wisdom," said Father loudly. I don't recall when I had ever seen him so happy.

Later, he told me that his work in the high school was exhausting. "But it's certainly going to change one of these days," he added. I did not ask if he was painting. It was a wound I dared not touch. Then he opened up to me, telling me about his studies in the academy and his long stay in Vienna. He spoke rapidly, as if trying to shorten a long tale. Because he hurried, I didn't understand very much, but his voice was penetrating, and there before my eyes were the stone, fortress-like buildings of the academy. I saw the art gallery that was part of it, with tall people walking about. I saw Father, too, dressed in a white suit, like the time we had gone together with Mother to the wedding of Felix Sommer, the artist. I remembered that wedding so well because it was on the banks of the Prut, and at the end of it I had been stung by a bee. Father went on talking and talking. I had never heard him talk so much, and so easily. Only after he's had a few drinks does he begin to loosen up. This time he must have overdone it. More than anything he said, I recall one gesture he made with his right hand, as if to say, "One day I'll remove the impediments and I'll be on my way." There was no anger in his face, only a steady determination.

And so we sat for about an hour. Then he told me things that I will never, ever forget: "Paul, my love, forgive me for not coming to visit you more frequently, but I've been trapped in that high school like a dog." I looked into his eyes, wide open and bloodshot, and it seemed to me that he was about to break a chair or a table. I was wrong. He lit a cigarette and chuckled to himself.

When we left the tavern Father's face shut down and his eyes narrowed, and all the way home he did not utter another sound. Our parting, as usual, was hasty, and he immediately disappeared.

I showed Halina my watch, and she said, "You have a very handsome father. Why did they divorce?"

"I don't know."

"Your father is a charming man."

I had heard the word "charming" more than once, but this time it did not sound pure to me. We sat by the table and watched the rain. In my imagination I saw Father running in the rain to catch the train, and I prayed silently that he would make it. The last train left at five o'clock.

Mother was late, and when she appeared in the doorway, I told her immediately that Father had been here and had brought me a watch.

"Wonderful," said Mother, and was silent. Apparently she hadn't expected him to come. "What did the two of you do?" she asked.

"Nothing much," I said, and didn't tell her that we had sat in a tavern and that Father had talked with great enthusiasm.

"So, what did you do?"

"We took a walk," I lied.

The lie weighed on me. Several times I almost admitted that I had lied. Father's surprise visit must have bothered her, for the following morning, she again asked, "So, what did you do?"

"Nothing much," I lied again.

I wore the watch and felt Father next to me. Since he brought me the watch, I could see his face clearly, and it seemed that any moment he'd come into my house.

"What does your father do?" Halina asked in a voice that carried an unpleasant ring.

"He teaches in high school," I hastened to answer. I didn't tell her about the painting. There were secrets that I wouldn't tell her, like the way Father drank and had difficulty painting. Sometimes I could feel the tremendous effort he made to save himself from his own silence, and I wanted to go to him and be near him. I knew that Mother wouldn't let me.

"Your father is a charming man," Halina said, as if to tease me.

"What is charming?" I pretended not to know.

"Don't you know?"

"No."

"Your father is a very handsome man, and all the women want to kiss him," she said, bursting into wild laughter and collapsing on the floor. Halina was lively and amusing but a chatterbox. After seven hours with her my head was full of noise, and I fled to the bedroom and curled up under the blanket so as to get away from it.

13

The days pass and Halina learns more and more German words. I'm embarrassed; my Ukrainian vocabulary is weak and jumbled, and I can hardly string a sentence together. When I finally come out with a Ukrainian sentence, Halina bursts out laughing, hugs and kisses me, and says that one of these days she'll take me to her village so that everyone can hear my accent.

"Is it a strange accent?"

"Extremely funny."

Halina's German sounds different from ours, but it's not funny—it has charm. I love to hear her ask a question or just say something. She tells me about her village and her parents. She seldom talks about her fiancé. She must understand that I don't like to hear about him.

A few days ago, she told me that her father would beat her when she was a child. Then she hitched up her dress and showed me the scars on her thigh. I was frightened: there were two long pinkish scars.

"Why did he beat you?"

"Because I was naughty."

"What did you do?"

"I would steal money and go to the store and buy chocolate."

"How often did he beat you?"

"Nearly every week."

"And you weren't afraid to steal?"

"I *was* afraid."

"So why didn't you stop?"

"Because I loved chocolate," she breathed, her nostrils flaring.

I love to listen to her voice. When she talks, her entire body speaks. Yesterday evening she told me that she would never forgive her father for beating her. "When I shouted, he would strangle me with his two hands."

From what she said, her mother was hardly blameless. "A bitter woman."

"They don't beat me," I bragged, perhaps unwisely.

"You're lucky. Jews don't beat their children."

"Why not?"

"I don't know."

We sit and talk for hours; so many amazing things have happened in Halina's life, and I want to hear more and more.

I hardly talk with Mother now. She returns home tired and distracted, and after dinner she settles down to grading homework. It's strange that she has hardly told me about her parents. Lately, I've meant to ask her about them, but when I see how distracted she is, I don't feel like doing so.

Eventually, when I summon the courage and ask, she says, "That's a long story, not for now. I'm so tired, I can barely keep my eyes open."

I'm angry with her, but I don't show it.

I sit and look at her. When I look at her, my love for her returns. I love her hair, her neck, and her way of leaning over the notebooks. I recall the long walks we took on our last vacation, the riverbanks, and the sandwiches we ate on the reed mat in the garden. I'm afraid that the closeness we shared will never be there again.

Mother lifts her head from the pile of notebooks. "You're not asleep yet, my love?"

"No."

"What are you thinking?"

"Nothing."

"Close your eyes and count to a hundred. I still have another pile of notebooks."

Before, Mother would have turned out the light and immediately gathered me in her arms, and I would have drifted into a deep sleep. But now she's preoccupied, and I find it hard to fall asleep. Thoughts devour my sleep. Even my dreams are not what they used to be. In dreams I see Halina, now as an angel and now as a demon; she tugs at my heart with magic powers and frightens me.

14

The days grew shorter and by four o'clock darkness fell outside our windows. We would spend most of the day sprawled on the floor, playing with dominos or wooden cubes, or rolling around under the beds. Halina knew how to be happy and how to entertain me. When the sun appeared from behind the clouds, we ran out to the candy store to buy a bar of chocolate. Every time Halina handed me the bar, I saw her father beating her with a thick belt, and I immediately offered her half. Halina refused my offer and said, "It's for you."

"For you, too." I extended the chocolate to her.

"Only one square."

"Don't you like chocolate?"

"Not that much now."

I asked her if I could cross the fence and enter the synagogue where the bearded Jews are.

"Why would you want to?" she asked, with a sour expression.

"I want to see how they pray."

"They don't pray nicely."

I climbed the fence easily and entered immediately. It was dark inside, and some bearded Jews sat around a long table. They seemed astonished to see me and looked me up and down. One of them came up to me and asked, "What's your name?"

I told him.

"And what's your Jewish name?"

"I don't know."

He put a skullcap on my head and said, "Come, sit with us."

They sat and sang with their eyes closed. Their singing was different from Mother's or Halina's. When they sang I felt that they were dredging up a viscous darkness from the bowels of the earth. And that is in fact what happened: the place was gradually filled with darkness, and the men on the benches cloaked themselves in it.

When they finished singing I wanted to return to Halina, but the man who had taken me to the table asked, "Where is your family from?"

I told him.

"And will you be staying here a long time?"

"Mother is a teacher at the school."

"Sit with us; we're going to sing some more," he said, and immediately started to sing.

These people did not look like us and were a little frightening, but for some reason I watched them closely and found myself drawn to them. At night they slipped into my dreams: an army of insects that devours everything in its path, even trees. Mother avoided them, Halina recoiled whenever we met one of them. To me, they sometimes seemed like one of the tribes that Mother told me about— the ones who sleep during the day and come awake at night, who love the moon and not the sun. The other tribes refer to them scornfully as "creatures of the night," but they are proud of their beliefs and claim that the light of the moon is more beautiful than the light of the sun, that it opens the heart to tranquillity and peace.

I left, and Halina was waiting for me outside. Her face was filled with anxiety and displeasure. "Why did you stay so long?"

"I listened to the singing."

"And what did they ask you?"

"They asked me my name."

"What else?"

"That's all."

"Don't go there anymore."

"Why?"

"They are not honest people."

Then she added, "They steal."

When Mother returned home I did not tell her that I had visited the bearded Jews.

I tell her very little these days, for I feel that her thoughts are elsewhere, and I repeatedly ask myself what she could be hiding from me. Sometimes it seems to me that she is drawing close to people whom she knew many years ago, but other times this impression recedes, and I see that her life is now free of Father's terror. Her gestures are more fluid, and she speaks freely, giving examples that make things understandable.

That evening I asked Mother, "Can I say that I'm a Jew?"

"To whom?"

"At the candy store."

"They know."

At night I dreamed that the bearded Jews tied me up me in the synagogue. I saw Halina and shouted for help, but she was clasped in her fiancé's embrace and didn't notice me. With all my might, I tried to free myself from my captors, but my arms were heavy, paralyzed. I awoke from sheer terror.

"What happened, my love?" Mother awoke, too.

"I was dreaming."

"Just disregard it," she said, as if it were unimportant, immediately falling back to sleep.

15

One evening a tall, blond man appeared at the door and Mother went to greet him. The man stared at me without saying a word. Mother's face filled with light and they began talking animatedly, as if they had known each other for a long time. I had never seen her speak to a strange man with such ease. They talked about school and about another man named Karol, a music teacher who was apparently rather stupid. I understood every word, and yet still the words seemed strange to me.

Only after they had spoken and laughed and made fun of Karol did Mother turn toward me and say, "This is André—he's the gym teacher at school." She wanted to show me off and said, impulsively, "Paul is already learning fractions, and he'll start percentages soon." André wrote an exercise for me, but I got muddled and it came out wrong, embarrassing both Mother and myself. Mother said, "He usually gets it right."

"Never mind, it happens," said André, rather tensely and without conviction.

I noticed that his blond hair was long, all the way down to his nape, and that his blue eyes had a cold glimmer to them. Mother was animated and laughing. Not since our vacation in the country had I seen her laugh like that.

"How old are you?" He turned to me.

I told him.

I was disappointed and angry that Mother was so very lively and so engaged in their conversation. I didn't say anything. I had already learned not to reveal my thoughts. A carefully guarded thought can be a pleasant secret.

I sat and looked at them for quite a while. Eventually I got tired of André's smooth face and sat down on the floor and played cards. Nothing is more enjoyable than cards. I pricked up my ears to catch what Mother was saying. She was using words she did not ordinarily use, such as "cutie" and "sweetie." I didn't like those words. I played a few more games and then I fell asleep. Beyond my sleep, I heard them chattering away happily and wanted to listen, but I was overcome with exhaustion.

The following day Mother got up late and rushed off to school. Her haste brought to mind André's smooth face and blond hair, and a wave of anger swept over me.

"How are you?" Halina asked when she arrived.

"André visited us," I told her.

"And what's he like?"

"Not that nice."

"But good-looking?"

"Not good-looking," I was about to say.

Then she said, "Your mother may be in love with him."

"Why do you say that?"

"That's how it seems to me."

Halina heard and knew everything. She knew that

Mother and Father divorced because Father was deeply depressed and addicted to alcohol, and that now he had also stopped making his alimony payments. I also knew that Mother and Father had divorced, but I didn't say this out loud. It seemed to me that this was a word that should not be spoken out loud.

"So, is André going to marry Mother?" The question popped out of my mouth.

"Possibly."

"Then I'll have a stepfather."

Halina told me something that surprised me. Her father, who had been so cruel to her, died when he was still young, and her mother married again. It turned out that the stepfather was more easygoing than her natural father. He simply ignored her. Halina often told me secrets from her own life. At seventeen there was already a lot of life in her body: rage at her dead father and scorn for her mother; while it was true that her mother didn't beat her with a belt, she would lash Halina with her tongue. "Sometimes the tongue hurts more than the strap," Halina told me.

Every word that came out of Halina's mouth went straight into me. I didn't always completely understand what she was saying, but I easily absorbed the sense of it, and at night when I was in bed I heard her voice and felt the touch of her hand.

My talks with Mother were now short and abrupt, and left nothing within me. She did not ask me very much, and I didn't ask her anything. It was as if our talks had been extinguished. Even at night, when I lay down next to her, I didn't think of her. I curled up in the corner of the bed, and whenever she touched me a shiver went down my back. Before I shut my eyes, Mother would ask me: "Wouldn't you like to go to school?"

"No."

"You won't be able to study in the high school."

"I don't care."

16

Halina also said that Mother had changed. She thought she was head over heels in love. I'd already noticed that Halina might not always have been sensitive, but her instincts were extremely sharp. She knew when it was going to rain and which birds forewarn of it. She once said, "It's not rain that will fall but hail." And she was right.

"What is love?" I asked her.

"Kissing," she said, and laughed.

"And what else?"

"You're still a child, you're too young to know."

"Tell me a bit."

"Well, you take off your clothes."

I saw Mother naked on our vacation. The lake was screened by dense foliage and we were alone. At first I was afraid of the quiet and of the gray water, but the moment we took off our clothes and immersed ourselves in the water, the fear receded. Toward evening we would get out and wrap ourselves up in large towels, shivering from the cold. Blueberry bushes grew along the road to our small house in the village, and we feasted on them, getting all stained.

I told Halina about that long, sweet summer. She listened and said, "We weren't taken on vacation. We started working when we were young."

I was sorry I had told her.

Later, I cried without knowing why. Halina asked me again and again, "Why are you crying?" I didn't know what to tell her. To cheer me up, she dressed me in my sailor outfit and we went out for a walk. Along the way, too, the tears welled up, but I kept them in.

Halina said to me, "You mustn't cry."

"Why?"

"Because it hurts more."

I think that she was right.

Now I was in no doubt: Mother was in love. Halina kept saying, "Your mother is in love." Perhaps she didn't mean to hurt me, but it did hurt. Mother was blossoming. I saw her happiness and my heart bled. André came again at night and Mother went out to meet him. He gave me another math exercise and again I became confused. Had it been in my power I would have thrown him out. Because I couldn't do that, I sat on the floor and played cards.

I woke up in the middle of the night and looked for Mother, but she wasn't next to me.

"Mother!" I called. Her side of the bed was a dark pit. I got up and went to the window. Trees rustled in the thick darkness. "Mother!" I called again and again, but she did not answer even this. The tears were about to burst out from within me, but I held them in. I remembered what Halina had taught me, and I curled up inside the blankets and pillows. "Mother loves André more than me," I murmured, choking back the tears. "I will never forget this betrayal, not even when I'm grown up."

As the darkness grew heavier, threatening to choke me, I heard the door opening. I knew it was Mother, but I closed my eyes and decided not to let her know that I had been awake and afraid. Without taking off her clothes, she lay down next to me. I felt her breathing and I knew that her eyes were open. Even when the dawn broke and there was light, I pretended that I was sleeping. Mother got up, changed her clothes, and sat at the mirror, putting on makeup, for a long time.

"How did you sleep?" Mother asked.

"Wonderfully."

"You didn't have any dreams?"

"No."

"Very good. I have to leave."

I was happy that she was going and that I would again be with Halina. At first I was about to tell Halina what had happened at night, but then I decided not to. It's better to keep a secret to yourself. When you tell a secret, you feel bad. But Halina didn't hold back that morning. She lashed out, angry at her fiancé, who had returned from the army without bringing her anything—not even a bar of chocolate.

"He must have another woman, I'm sure of it," she said, clenching her jaw.

"How do you know?"

"The smell. I smelled perfume on his body."

"And what did he say?"

"He denies it, swears it's not true. But I don't believe his oaths."

"So you won't marry him?"

"No."

When Halina was angry at her fiancé she was more beautiful. Her tanned face glowed and her eyes flashed.

17

Suddenly the sun came out, and in the yard next to us the bearded Jews were wearing white.

"What's going on?" I asked Halina.

"It's the Jewish New Year today, didn't you know?"

"No."

Halina had worked for religious Jews, and she knew lots about them; she was always telling me interesting details.

"On Rosh Hashanah they dip an apple in honey so it'll be a sweet new year."

"And why do they wear white clothes?"

"To look like angels."

"You're teasing me."

"No."

I had already noticed: sometimes Halina looked at them with a hidden smile; she worked for them for two years, and those days are ingrained in her memory.

Halina put the sailor cap on my head, and I went into the synagogue. At first no one paid any attention to me. But after a short while, I found myself surrounded by people. Now they seemed very tall to me. One of them put a prayer shawl around my shoulders and said, "It's a tallis." The shawl was not heavy, but it was cold, and it made me shiver.

They must know everything about us, for I heard one of them say, "He's a Jew, he's a Jew for sure." Then he leaned down, held out a prayer book, and said, "This is a siddur."

"What should I do with it?" I raised my eyes.

"Hold it."

I clasped it to my heart and stood there. The men wrapped themselves in prayer shawls and prayed with devotion, and for a moment it seemed that God was looking down from the ceiling, and I lowered my eyes.

Then I left, and no one stopped me. It seemed that the praying grew stronger and could be heard in our backyard. The thought that I, too, was Jewish and that I was also allowed to pray made me glad for a moment. I revealed my thought to Halina.

"You want to be like the bearded Jews?" Halina wondered.

The direct question confused me, and I said, "No." Then I regretted it and said, "Still, they do pray nicely."

Of course, I didn't say anything to my mother; she can't stand them. She once said to me, "They speak so loudly and dress in such a slovenly way." Since then, I've been careful not to ask her about them. Truth be told, I was drawn to them. Sometimes I felt that I'd been with them before, that I'd even taken part in their prayers, but where and when I did not remember. Halina said, "After all, you are only nine years old, you can't remember," and she must be right.

Sometimes my memory played tricks on me. For example, I didn't recall Father ever raising his voice or shouting. Halina said that before divorcing, people shout at each other, and even come to blows. She didn't know that Father was a quiet person, that he may have clenched his jaws, but he wouldn't let a loud word out of his mouth. Sometimes she asked me about Father, but I didn't tell her the truth. Her questions about Father were far from innocent. "He's a good-looking man, all the girls are attracted to him," she whispered.

Once again I tried to draw her out, asking her to tell me about the bearded Jews. Halina didn't always want to talk about them. Three weeks had already passed since her fiancé went back to the army, and there was no word from him.

"He's not serving far from home," she railed. "If he wanted to, he could have come. His army friends go home at night and return the next day."

"You're angry with him?"

"Very."

"And you won't marry him?"

"No."

If Halina didn't marry, she'd be with me forever. I curled up inside this thought, happy.

The day came that everyone calls Yom Kippur. It was a cold and clear evening, and upon all the backyards a frozen quiet descended. Jews in white clothing hurried to the synagogue, and Ruthenian women stood leaning against the fences, watching them closely. Halina and I also stood next to our fence. Halina's face was serious, and I saw how the awe of this evening was upon her, too.

"What is Yom Kippur?"

"I'll explain it to you soon."

The synagogue doors were open, and candles lit up the wide entranceway. You couldn't see the faces of those praying—they were wrapped in prayer shawls, weeping. "What's going on?" I asked, but Halina was involved with her own soul and paid no attention to me. It seemed to me that there would soon be a loud noise, and lightning would split the sky. It wasn't so. The evening was clear and quiet, and the longer the sunset lingered on into dusk, the more intense the silence became. The Ruthenian women, too, remained standing by their fences without moving, as if a spell had been cast upon them.

After this, the restrained weeping turned into long and drawn-out sobbing. Halina lifted up her head and said, "I don't know why, but this evening always moves me." Tears welled up in her eyes. And so we stood there for a long time. The wonder faded slightly, but I felt that this evening would long remain with me, even after I grew up.

We went inside. Halina lit a lantern and said, "These Jews always amaze me." In what way, I wanted to ask but did not.

Mother returned late. Her face was covered with weariness and indifference, as if her secret had been snatched from her. I wanted to feel pity for her, but my heart wouldn't let me. I remembered the black night and how I had called out, "Mother, Mother!" and I immediately felt estranged from her.

18

Father appeared immediately after Yom Kippur. His expression frightened me, and I clung to Halina's legs. Father's face had grown darker since I last saw him. He was wearing a long raincoat and a black peaked cap, and he carried a bag in his right hand. "Father!" I called, without letting go of Halina. On hearing my cry, he bent down and stretched out his arms to me. I detached myself from Halina and went to him.

Once again, we crossed and recrossed the main street in silence. Father wanted to say something, but the words stuck in his throat. Father is tall and strong—he can lift tables and chests of drawers—but he finds talking difficult. When he's angry he smashes things, but he doesn't lash out at people. Once I saw him break a chair into pieces. Mother stood by the door without uttering a sound. From then on I knew that he must not be annoyed.

We sat in the café we used to go to. To break the silence, I told him about my walks with Halina, about the ice-cream shop and the candy kiosks. Father listened but he was not with me; his thoughts were elsewhere. The waitress brought him a cup of coffee and me a hot chocolate. His face had become more wrinkled, and I saw that his thoughts gave him no rest.

When he finished the coffee, Father began talking with pent-up anger about a certain man who had just been appointed curator of the municipal museum, a Dr. Manfred Zauber, who once wrote a scathing review of his paintings. I gazed into his blazing eyes and saw the fire burning in them.

Later, we sat in the tavern. Father talked about the delays and the obstacles that kept him from painting. He had never talked with me about his paintings. Now his words rolled out of his mouth like heavy stones. I was afraid to look at him. After a few drinks he relaxed, spoke with the waitress, and complimented her. The waitress confided that she would soon be leaving this backwater and going to Czernowitz. Life in the provinces depressed her; it was better in a large city—you've got cinemas and nightclubs there. Father looked at her as if to say, "I hope you won't be disappointed."

On the way home he asked me if I had seen Mother's new friend.

"No," I lied.

"Your mother has a boyfriend, and his name is André." Father rolled the *r* with a strange emphasis. I glanced at his face and was afraid that he would go on questioning me, but he didn't. His face got tighter and tighter, and he looked like a man rushing to get somewhere. At the house he hugged me and said, "Hurry on in!" Then he immediately turned away.

I stood watching him for a long time. I was sure that at any moment he would smash the gate of the municipal park and the wooden platform where the fire-brigade band played every Sunday. I stood and waited for the noise of wood smashing, and when it didn't come, I went inside.

It was already late, and Mother hadn't arrived yet. Halina didn't ask how it went. We sat on the floor and began to play cards. Most of the time I'm lucky and I win.

This time Halina won. Whenever she won, a malicious grin spread across her face, as if she were saying, "Don't I also deserve to win sometimes?"

I said nothing about what Father had told me. Whenever she said, "Your father," it was with a wicked smile on her lips. In the end, she couldn't contain herself and said, "Your father is a good-looking man; all the girls are in love with him." It was clear to me that she counted herself among them, but she was careful not to say it.

Later I asked her if she believed in God.

"Of course I believe," she said, kissing the crucifix on the chain around her neck.

"Why doesn't Mother believe in God?"

"She's a teacher."

"Teachers don't believe in God?"

"Only Jewish teachers."

"But the bearded Jews believe in God."

"They? Yes."

The conversation confused me.

Mother arrived later, apologized, and said, "Our staff meeting took longer than usual."

I did not believe her.

19

It rained incessantly, and we sat on the broad bed playing cards. For an instant it seemed that it would be like this forever, and I wasn't sorry. Halina was amazed by my victories—when she was amazed at me she hugged me and kissed me and called me her sweetie. She was wild and her embraces could hurt, but mostly they were pleasant.

Mother was so distracted and confused that sometimes she called me Arthur, my father's name—last night she did it again. Not only were her thoughts scattered, but her movements, too. From time to time, a saucepan or a glass would slip from her hands. Yesterday she dropped a stack of plates. Seeing the pieces, she knelt down, covered her face, and said, "What's happening to me? Everything's slipping through my fingers."

When I was just about to fall asleep, Mother asked, "How is Father?"

"He's all right." I didn't mean what I said.

"What did you do?"

"We sat in a tavern." I let her in on something I need not have told her.

Mother came over to me and, with a catch in her

throat, said, "You mustn't go into a tavern. A tavern is a dangerous place."

"Why?" An impish devil egged me on.

"People get drunk in taverns," she said, and burst into tears. She sat on the bed and cried for a long time, but I felt no pity for her. I was sure that she was not crying for Father or even for me, but for herself.

Since she had started coming back late, only to disappear at night, I have been repulsed by her. Even her clothes, which I used to love to smell, put me off—they were now saturated with a suffocating perfume, and I was glad that Halina crammed them into the chest of drawers in the morning.

"What's the matter?" Mother sometimes asked.

"Nothing," I said without meeting her gaze.

Once I loved hearing her read aloud from a book. Even now she forced me to listen to her reading. But I didn't listen to her, I only looked at her lips and told myself, "These lips that kiss André in the dark are not clean lips. I'd far rather have Halina's kisses, because she hates her fiancé and she loves me."

On my last outing with Halina we got as far as the Jewish orphanage, on the outskirts of the city. We stood next to the high fence for a while. Everything there looked rundown, peeling, and neglected, and the children's faces were sickly and jaundiced. Halina told me that if a child had no father or mother, he was sent there.

"But I have parents," I hastened to say.

"True," Halina said.

Yet I couldn't shake off the feeling that soon I would also be sent to the orphanage. I did not tell her about that feeling. I had begun to be haunted by a different fear. I dreamed that André was punishing me the way the Ruthenians punish their children. First they make them bend over, and then they strip off their pants. The children scream and try to escape, but it's useless—the belt comes down on them time after time, and the father won't stop thrashing until he draws blood.

Mother abandoned me every night so she could go to André. The darkness frightened me, but I swore to myself that I was not going to cry. I sat on the bed or stood by the window. Sometimes I armed myself with two kitchen knives, so that if the darkness invaded, I could thrust into it, wounding it on the spot. Halina had told me something else: that Jews do not marry non-Jews. When I asked her if André was Jewish, she laughed and said, "He's a goy—you know what a goy is?"

"No."

"Whoever isn't a Jew is a goy. Not a nice word—don't use it."

Mother, it seemed, had no idea that I was awake during the nights, that I heard her dressing and leaving stealthily and returning toward morning. She thought that I didn't know what she did at night, but I knew everything. Halina had already told me and made me swear that I wouldn't tell a soul. After they kiss, they would undress and stick to each other when they were naked. I had complete faith in what Halina said. Halina didn't lie to me like Mother did. Since she had told me this secret, it had been hard for me to speak to Mother. I had nothing but scorn for her, and I swore to myself that as soon as I grew up I would not see her face anymore.

20

Catastrophes come when you least expect them. While we were sitting and playing cards on the broad bed, enjoying the warmth of the stove, eating cheese pastries filled with raisins, playing, laughing, and fooling around, a man's shadow appeared at the entrance of the house. He knocked on the door. At first it seemed that this had to be someone who was lost and found his way here by accident, but the shadow stayed stuck to the door and the fist continued to rap on it.

"Who's there?" asked Halina.

The man said his name and Halina opened the door. As it turned out, it was a soldier, Halina's fiancé. The fiancé was not happy and did not embrace her but immediately began to ask her questions in a loud voice. Halina answered but must have become confused. The fiancé became angry and raised his voice. Halina rallied and spoke in a flood of words. He interrupted her and silenced her. Halina ticked off on her fingers everything that she had done in the past few days, but he shouted, "Shut up, you liar!"

"You're the liar!" she burst out to his face. "You've got another woman in the village!"

"You'll speak to me with respect!" He turned on her in a choked voice.

"I'm not afraid, you're not my husband," she said defiantly.

"I'm your fiancé, so mind your language."

"I'll do as I please."

"You certainly won't!"

"I will."

"You will not."

"Get out of here, this isn't your house!" she screamed at him.

When he heard this last pronouncement of hers, he loaded his rifle and took aim. It was a very strong shot, and it shook the house. Immediately there was silence. Halina fell to the floor with a groan. The neighbors burst in. The fiancé made a dash for it, slipping away as the neighbors shouted, "Catch the murderer!"

"Murder! Murder!" everyone was shouting. In no time at all, the police arrived, accompanied by the doctor and a medic. The doctor knelt down and exclaimed, "She's wounded! Take her to the hospital at once."

"Is she breathing?" the women in the doorway asked.

The doctor ignored them. He and the medic carried Halina to the open cart outside, laid her on the flat surface with her arms dangling, and were off at once.

"God, spare Halina!" I cried, breaking down. Meanwhile, there were people all over the house. Everyone knew that Halina had already been taken to the hospital, and yet they stood there as if rooted to the spot, as if a secret was still lurking within. The news spread rapidly and reached the school. Soon Mother pushed her way through the crowd and hurried toward me. André was with her, which stripped the meeting of all emotion.

Mother did not ask, "What happened? What did you see?" as once she would have. She just stood there and explained to André about Halina's life. I was hurt that she could tell him things that were only for us and Halina. I was about to shout, "Shut up!" but didn't dare. I moved aside and went into the bedroom. I saw the disheveled bed where we had been romping about a short while ago, and my heart tightened and my legs trembled.

Mother and André were engrossed in their conversation and didn't even look for me. "God, give me back Halina!" I cried out, feeling pain in my stomach. The pain spread to my thighs and stayed there. And for a moment it seemed to me that Halina was hiding beneath the bed, as she used to do. I lifted the cover and bent down carefully. The musty darkness assaulted my nostrils.

I told myself that Halina was in a deep sleep and that the doctors were taking care of her. Last spring, Father and Mother had taken me to the hospital to have my tonsils removed. They had been inflamed and had hurt me the entire winter. Father had said, "It will be as easy as removing a hair from a glass of milk."

I had believed him. A short time after that one of the doctors, a large, strong woman, had put a mask over my face and suffocated me. I don't remember anything of the operation, only the suffocation before it and the pain that followed it, and the ice cream that Mother fed me. The ice cream had looked wonderful but didn't taste good. I could taste the medication in it.

I envisioned Halina lying in bed and one of the nurses giving her ice cream. Halina tells her about the pain and the nurse explains to her that the ice cream heals like medicine. I got into bed and covered my head with the blanket. I immediately felt more certain that Halina would get better and that, in a short while and to everyone's astonishment, she would rise, like Jesus, and come to me.

21

I slept until late morning. When I woke up, Mother said, "I'll be leaving for school soon. There are sandwiches and drinks in the pantry; you'll have to look after yourself."

"Where is Halina?"

"In the hospital."

"When is she coming back?"

"Let's hope she recovers."

Only when Mother had gone to school and I was all alone did I again see Halina as she fell to the floor. Everything spun around me.

I went outside. The garden was quiet, illuminated by the muted morning light. I approached the fence between us and the bearded Jews. An elderly man came up to me and asked how I was. I told him that the day before, Halina's fiancé had wounded her and now she was lying in the hospital.

"And who's looking after you?" he asked with concern.

"I'm on my own, but I'm not afraid."

The old man smiled and said, "God will look after you."

He held me in his gaze, and I felt as if he knew not only what had taken place the day before, but all that had happened to us since Father had left the house and we arrived here. I wanted to enter the synagogue and pray for Halina, but I didn't dare. So I locked up the house and went into the street, thinking that I'd make my way to the hospital. On our walks outside the city, Halina had once pointed out a low structure, saying, "That's the municipal hospital." The building was hardly welcoming; it resembled the orphanage. The forecourt was neglected and some Ruthenian horses harnessed to miserable carriages stood around listlessly, as if they had lost all will to live.

I knew the main street and some of the side streets well; I'd spent so many hours walking with Halina. Now the sidewalks were drowning in fallen leaves, and I waded through them. I passed the tavern and thought of Father. Now I often saw Father in my dreams. In a dream his silence is more tangible. A black flame flickers in his eyes and his lips are pursed. Once I asked him in a dream why he doesn't speak. He looked at me with his black eyes and said, "That's how it is." He often said that.

The gate and the front door of the hospital were open, and it was easy to enter. The main corridor was empty, and so was the corridor that led off it. At the end of the corridors there were steps, and I went up them.

"Who are you looking for?" a man in orange overalls addressed me.

"I'm looking for Halina," I replied immediately.

"Go to the information counter," he said, and turned away.

The information counter, it turned out, was right alongside me. The man there glanced at me and asked, "Who are you, son?"

I told him.

"Halina has had two operations, and we have to pray for her recovery."

"When can I see her?"

"When the Almighty will open her eyes."

It was eleven o'clock, but I was in no hurry to return home. The man's answers sounded unclear but not without hope, perhaps because he had mentioned God. I passed the orphanage and remembered what Halina had said to me about the place. Then I stopped at the home of Princess Josephina, which is surrounded by a large garden and has a high iron gate in front. Halina had told me a lot about the princess, who was related to the royal family and was now living there by herself. At each step I could hear Halina, even by the trees at the post office. Next to the post office she once told me, "Only letters leave here, never people. People get stuck here forever."

At the chapel next to the post office I saw a woman kneeling and praying, and for a moment I told myself that I would also kneel and pray for Halina's recovery. But it was a long line and the people who were waiting did not look nice.

I didn't return home until one o'clock. I did not touch the sandwiches that Mother had left. The empty house seemed to me like a body without a soul. Halina had taught me that a person's soul is in the middle of his chest, but you can't see it because it's pure spirit. When a man dies, his soul ascends to heaven and merges with Jesus. One mustn't be afraid of death because death is light and not darkness. That's what Halina taught me.

Mother returned late and brought me a gift: a cotton shirt and gym shoes. I should have thanked her and been happy, but I was angry with her and with her red lips. Whenever she left the house she put lipstick on her lips and reeked of perfume.

I burrowed into the bed and covered my head with the blankets.

"Aren't you going to eat dinner?" Mother asked in an affected tone of voice.

"I'm very tired," I said, and closed my eyes.

I knew that at midnight, after she had graded the notebooks, she would get dressed and leave the house. This certainty did not hurt me now—my hatred was stronger than the pain, and it drugged my sleep.

22

Mother leaves every morning, and I stay home alone. Without Halina, the house is cold and gloomy, and I leave it as soon as I can. First I cross the main street and then I immediately turn into the alley that leads to the municipal hospital. Sometimes I forget about Halina and roam aimlessly, but when I reach the street where the hospital is and see the neglect there and the homeless lying under the awning, I quickly climb the steps, go up to the information counter, and ask how Halina is. It doesn't take long to hear the answer: "May God have mercy."

When I hear the voice of the man at the desk, I imagine that the doctors who have looked after Halina until now have taken off their white coats, put on priestly robes, and are now kneeling by her bed every hour in prayer. Once in the corridor I saw a peasant couple sitting on the bench. I was sure that they were Halina's mother and stepfather, but it turned out that I was wrong. The woman had come to see the doctor; she registered at the information counter, and her husband paid for the visit.

Most of the day I wander along the side streets and alleys. I have stolen a little money from Mother's purse, and I buy two overflowing cones of ice cream at a time. An ice-cream cone brings to mind running in the rain with Halina along the main road from the ice-cream shop to the house. It wouldn't help that we made a dash for it—we would still get soaked. Halina would immediately strip off my wet clothes and dress me in dry ones. These fumbled actions filled me with sensations of rain and laundry starch.

Those are the pleasant, fleeting memories. Mostly I see the gushing wound in Halina's neck. The doctors are helpless, and whenever her condition worsens, they get down on their knees and pray. At these times I also want to get down on my knees in the corridor, to pray together with the doctors. Sometimes I think I see Father coming toward me. I haven't seen him for weeks. I used to envision him walking with people. Now I see him alone, his loneliness trailing after him like a long shadow. I feel his presence grow within me; now I've come to know his long strides, the way he holds a glass, and the way he grips his old duffel bag. When I reach his age, I'm sure I'll be as silent as he is.

One night I dream that I stole money from Mother's purse and took a train to visit Father. At the station I asked where he lived. I was happy, because everyone knew him and told me how to get to him. Then I wake up and Mother is not next to me. Darkness lies curled up where she had been.

So now Mother sleeps with André and she's warm. I'm cold and long shadows hover about, deceiving me. Never mind—when Halina recovers, I'll run away to her village with her. In the country there are fields and streams, and we'll take walks from morning till late at night.

Mother comes back from school and asks, "What did you do?"

"I played."

"You weren't bored?"

"No."

"I'm looking for a woman to come and look after you, but I can't find one."

"You don't have to."

"Why?"

"I'm waiting for Halina."

"Halina is very ill."

"She'll soon be well."

"Who knows."

Once, I adored Mother's voice; now every word grates. When she talks about Halina, she says, "Perhaps . . . Possibly . . . Who knows?" If she really loved me, she would not speak like that, she would use different words. But because she loves André and not me, she uses words that André uses—dry words like the blond hair that comes down to his neck.

I go to the hospital every day, and I prepare myself to run away with Halina to her village. I keep my plan totally secret. The thought that I will be in her village in just a few days makes me so happy that I begin to skip in the street, and I have the feeling that no one can catch me.

The brief talks with Mother at night are forced and wearying, and I'm happy that she leaves me alone and sits at the table, correcting notebooks. Sometimes her face takes on a light from days past, and I remember her beauty. This, of course, is just an illusion. She has changed so much. Her hands have broadened and she eats hastily, buttering slice after slice, trying to get me to eat. I don't feel like taking part in this fit of eating that's called dinner. I sit to one side and stare at her, and the more I look at her, the more I know that this is not the mother that I loved.

One day I walk by the school and see the children in the

school yard fighting and shouting, and I am so happy that I am not learning there that I forget about Halina and walk all the way to the orphanage, telling myself, "Father knows what's best for me." Because Father had saved me by the magic of a single word: "asthma."

As I approach the hospital, I suddenly think that I also need to use magic, so I can pull Halina out of the deep sleep into which she has fallen.

23

I'm on my own for the time being, and happy. But when I suddenly remember Halina lying in the hospital, I brush aside my thoughts and run there. Again, the man at the information counter says, "May God have mercy," as if there are no other words in the world. One day I summon up the courage to ask, "Can I see Halina?"

"She's sleeping and mustn't be disturbed," he says, placing a finger to his lips. His answer raises my spirits, and I retreat on tiptoe. In the hospital forecourt a group of homeless have gathered, arguing, shouting, and making a great deal of noise. "You aren't allowed to shout here," I want to tell them. For the rest of that day, until evening, I am aware of Halina's sleep, walking carefully so as not to make a noise.

In the evening Mother asks, "How was your day?" Of course I do not tell her anything.

The next day I go into the synagogue next door. There is only one man in the place, and he asks me what I want.

"To pray," I answer.

"It's late. We've already prayed."

"I'd like to learn how to pray," I explain.

On hearing this, his lips crease into a smile and he says,

"You first have to learn the letters." He immediately takes down a prayer book and shows me the large letters. He points to the first letter and says, *"Alef."* Then, seeming to remember that he hasn't asked, he inquires, "Why do you want to pray?"

"Halina is very sick."

He apparently does not understand me, for he says, "First you have to learn the letters."

"I want to learn."

"Tell your mother to send you to the *cheyder.*"

I feel that he still doesn't understand me, and I am about to leave.

"Who are you?" He again turns to me.

I tell him my name.

My name seems to tell him nothing, for he asks no more and turns away from me.

I understand that this might not be the right person to speak to, and I leave.

The desire to pray grows stronger in me, and I walk on till I find myself at the chapel. The tiny chapel can hold no more than one person at a time. When there isn't a line, the person coming to pray can take his time, but if there is a line, he hurries his prayers and then blesses the person coming after him. It's mostly women who come here, but I've also seen men. Once I saw a tall, strong man kneeling and shaking the small wooden structure.

And so the days pass. Sometimes I sense that Halina's sleep is dragging her into a deep gorge and that someone must hasten to pull her out. I shared this feeling with the man at the information counter. He smiled and said, "It's absolutely forbidden to wake her up." Since he said that to me, my life has become smaller.

Now I hardly ask, and I just wander along the side streets. When this tires me, I curl up in bed and sleep for several hours.

"I can't find a woman to look after you," Mother says in an empty voice on her return.

"There's no need," I answer coldly.

"You aren't bored?" Again, that superficial voice.

"No."

Once Mother would have told me stories or read to me or sat quietly by my side. Now it seems that it's not her sitting next to me but another woman. My real mother has slipped away and left me with this awful substitute, and every word that comes out of her mouth wounds me. Sometimes I want to shout out, "You're not my mother!" I contain the fury in my heart by telling myself, "It's better that I hold it in; in only a few days Halina will wake up from her sleep and I'll run away with her."

It gets colder each day, and in the morning frost glitters on the grass. But this doesn't stop me from going to the hospital every day. Sometimes I think that the man at the information counter understands me and wants to help me, but the nurses, who wear yellow uniforms, refuse to cooperate.

Every evening, Mother's mindless chatter makes my blood boil. For some reason, she's sure that Halina won't return to us. Too many days have passed since she lost consciousness. She calls Halina's sleep "a loss of consciousness," and to me that sounds as if she's refusing to believe that Halina will come back. "She'll come back soon," I say, not hiding my confidence from her.

Mother says, "It's not good to harbor illusions"—words she has already used. They grated on my ears then, too.

Since she has been teaching at the school Mother uses words that she didn't use before. Like "to harbor," and "treatment and development," and other words that freeze my heart. Mother would correct Halina's German, but I loved the timbre of her voice and the way she pronounced the words. When she said, "Come, let's put on your coat," I felt that the two of us would wrap ourselves in it and that no one else would see us, but that we would see everyone.

24

Day after day, fierce rain continues to fall, and it's hard to get to the hospital. The water rushes down the streets, drawing mud with it. At times the rain becomes hail and lashes my face. I have a raincoat and boots that cover my feet, but I rarely use an umbrella. The umbrella comes between me and the sky, between me and people in the street. It's better to get wet and be able to see than to walk like a blind person—that's what I learned from Father. Father has a large umbrella, but he seldom uses it.

After visiting the hospital, I wander for about three or four hours and return home soaked, but there is something special to this dampness. I sleep differently. In my dreams I run with Halina. Running with Halina is brisk and joyful, and, as she always does after we run in the rain, she strips off my wet clothes and puts me in dry ones.

I've noticed that in recent days Mother returns early and prepares a huge dinner. After that she sits and talks to me about school. She is not in a hurry, and she seems calmer and less distracted. What has happened? I'm suspicious and prick up my ears. Sometimes André comes and joins our meal.

One evening Mother raises her head, looks at me, and says, "I want to tell you something."

"What?"

"André and I have decided to get married."

"When?"

"Soon. Are you angry?"

"No."

I had known that a heavy blow would come but had no idea from where. I get up, go over to the sideboard, take out my wooden balls from the drawer, and put them on the floor. Halina brought me these balls from the village, and we would play with them for hours. I haven't touched them for a while, but now it seems to me that they bear a secret, that they can be trusted. I start rolling them, just as Halina taught me.

Later Mother asks me, "Would you like to be at the wedding ceremony?"

"I don't know."

"You don't have to."

We don't talk more that night. I sit on the floor and roll the balls. The thought that Halina will soon be well and that I will run away with her to her village gives me secret joy, like a sweet dream. Mother grades her notebooks and I play. I know that this night, too, I will hear her footsteps as she slips away. She will walk on her tiptoes, open the door carefully, and muffle the creaking. These sharp and tense moments wound me: I feel intensely sorry for myself and want to cry. Once I had a mother. That was long ago, for now she belongs to André. She gets undressed and they kiss each other and roll on the bed. This knowledge drives me mad, and I want to shout "Murder!"—just as the neighbors shouted when they saw Halina weltering in her blood. I feel sorry for my father; he wastes all his money on drink. He doesn't even have the money to visit me. He must know that Mother is about to marry and so he drinks even more. "Father!" I call out. For an instant, the darkness trembles and shadows flee from the walls. I am sure that Father has heard my cry and that he will come and visit me soon. Whenever I really long for him, he comes.

25

Mother returned toward dawn. She took off her clothes, put on a nightdress, and lay down next to me. I turned my back to her so she couldn't look at me. I didn't like it when she looked at me or hugged me.

In the morning she hurried off to school and barely kissed me. I remembered the long summer vacation we spent together on the shores of the Prut, and my heart bled. Now, instead of that closeness there were just some blurred patches of memory and a feeling of uncleanliness.

Sometimes I felt that Mother wanted to crawl out of her skin and come back to me, but she was trapped inside the movements she had picked up from André. She called them her flexibility exercises. But it was hopeless—they really didn't suit her. She must have been exercising with him, or who knew what. I, at any rate, made my peace with the fact that she was no longer my mother. I was very upset that she pretended that nothing had happened and she said, "In the winter we'll travel to the Carpathians and we'll go skiing." I hoped that in winter I'd be very far from her and her lies.

In the meantime, the rains ceased and low mist-like clouds crawled between the houses and the alleys; the wetness seeped into everything. I wanted to go into the café and sit amid the tobacco smoke, as I used to sit with Halina not so long ago. Halina had said something to me then that stayed in my mind: "Jews are hardworking and that's why they do well."

"And will I also do well?" I hastened to ask.

"I don't doubt it for a moment," she said, and chuckled.

She also laughed when she told me about injustice and pain.

Without being aware of it, I had reached the hospital. The forecourt was empty, but beneath the awning the homeless and the drunks had gathered. They immediately spotted me and shouted, "Here's the Jewish dwarf!" I was surprised; I had never been called anything like this before, and I wanted to laugh, but I understood soon enough that it wasn't a joke. A stone was thrown, and it hit my thigh. I wanted to run away, but my legs told me to seek shelter in the building, and that's what I did.

"How is Halina?" I asked the man at the information counter and waited for his usual answer.

"She is no longer in pain." He leveled his gaze at me.

"Is she better?"

"She's already in heaven," he said, and removed his cap from his head.

I did not know what his look meant, and I stared at him.

"She's already in heaven," he repeated in a soft voice.

I then understood, but I didn't want to understand. "She's still sleeping?" I asked.

"She's already with God, my child. She can no longer suffer. Do you understand me?"

"I understand."

"The good Father will look after her."

"Thank you," I said in utter confusion.

"For something like this we don't give thanks," he said, and looked away.

I went quickly down the staircase and crossed the forecourt. It started raining again, and I felt the wetness in the soles of my feet, but I wasn't cold. I walked in the direction of the orphanage, meaning to reach the post office. There's an awning at the post office where you can take shelter from the rain. What I'd just heard had already made its way into me, but I did not yet feel it. I was hungry and thought about a cheese sandwich. The post office was full of people, so I immediately headed toward the kiosk where Halina used to buy me sandwiches filled with yellow cheese. The kiosk owner asked me my name, and I told him.

"You're Jewish?" He chuckled.

"True."

"Do you speak Yiddish?"

"No."

"Too bad."

There were bearded Jews like him in the synagogue next to our house. He gave me the sandwich and said, "May God bless you."

I didn't know what to say, so I said, "Thank you."

The man looked at me and for a moment it seemed that he was about to say, "For something like this we don't give thanks." The sandwich didn't taste good, but I wolfed it down anyway. It was still raining, and I decided to return home. I was sure that if I went home, I would see that a miracle had occurred.

As I entered the house, I saw no change at all. Mother's clothes were scattered on the bed and on the chest of drawers. Even my few clothes were strewn on the sideboard. I recalled Mother's hasty departure and anger welled up inside me. I took off the wet clothes and felt better. I went into the kitchen and then went back to the bedroom. For a moment it seemed to me that were I to stand still and eavesdrop, I might hear a voice. And then I really did hear Halina's voice laughing and saying, "The Jews are hardworking and because of this, they do well. Ruthenians are lazy and they waste all their money on drink. They don't know how to live. If they knew how to live, they would leave the country."

There was no doubt it was Halina's laugh. I went over to the window to see if she was in the garden or in the pantry. It was open, and the garden was wet from the rain. There was no one there. A few birds were perched silently on the fence. In the background I saw the clouds and the drunks under the awning shouting at me, "Jewish dwarf!"

26

I must have slept for some time. When I awoke, Mother was already poring over her notebooks. "You haven't eaten anything," she said to me. "Should I prepare something for you?"

"I'm not hungry," I said without lifting my head from the pillow. I heard her leave the house, and I heard her return toward morning.

I woke up early and got dressed. Only now did my thigh hurt from the stone that had hit me, and for a moment I was about to tell Mother, but I bit my tongue. We ate a hasty breakfast. On her way to the door, Mother muttered a few words and I heard her say the name Halina. I wanted to ask what happened, but she slipped away and was gone.

I was afraid to stay at home, so I went out. At first I thought of going to the hospital, but I changed my mind and went to the chapel where I had often been with Halina. Once, one of the women there had told us, "You can't stand here watching. You can't watch people when they're praying."

Halina had answered whatever she answered, but we continued to come, perhaps because I dragged Halina there.

This time there was no one inside. The chapel door was

wide open, and the icon gazed out from it. I hesitated but finally went in and knelt down. The tortured man in the icon stared at me, and I closed my eyes. I felt dizzy, and I covered my face with my hands.

I went back downtown and saw Halina floating in the sky, as if in a vision. She was wearing an embroidered blouse, a linen skirt, and sandals. She was very real and yet still distant. Once, in one of the icons, I saw someone floating like this. I asked Father what the floating meant, and he answered briefly, "After his death, Jesus went up to heaven."

I continued walking in the direction of the ice-cream shop. I no longer saw Halina. I bought one ice-cream cone and then immediately bought another one. My pockets were full of money, and I spent it carelessly.

In the evening Mother told me that Halina had passed away and that there would be a funeral in her village in three days' time. "Has passed away" means going to heaven, I told myself. I did not ask for details, so as not to let her know that I was waiting for Halina to come back to me. Later, Mother asked how I was and how I had spent the time. The question and the way she asked it made me furious. Since she'd started slipping off to be with André at night, she either talked to me in a pretentious tone or smothered me with embraces.

Before she started correcting her notebooks at the table, she asked if I would like to go to the funeral.

"I have to be there," I said in a strong voice.

Mother appeared to be very taken aback by my reply, and she asked me why. My hands trembled, and I wanted to pick up a chair and smash it; I restrained myself and said in a clear voice, "I want to see Halina going to heaven." Mother looked as though she was about to reply, but she didn't. I was very agitated and couldn't fall asleep. Mother began to correct the notebooks, but every few minutes she turned to me and asked, "Aren't you asleep yet?" I didn't bother answering. Every answer drew an annoying response; it was best not to talk. In the end I pretended to sleep.

At night after Mother had left, I could hold it in no longer and I shouted, "Halina, come quickly! I can't take these lies any longer!"

The days till the funeral crawled by. I ate many sandwiches and a lot of ice cream and even a bar of Suchard chocolate that I bought at the patisserie. I took the money from my back pocket and paid. It was a pity Halina wasn't with me—we could have celebrated together.

"How come you've got so much money?" asked the Jew at the patisserie.

"Mother gave it to me."

"You shouldn't carry so much money in your pockets."

"Why?"

"Money isn't a good thing."

Now I realized: this Jew knew my sin, and it would be best to make myself scarce there. And that's what I did, but the fear stayed with me. Halina told me that thieves are locked up in narrow cells at the prison, and once a day they're beaten so that they won't forget what they've done.

27

We traveled to the funeral in the afternoon. Mother had rented a horse-drawn carriage, and it brought us to the village. Mother was wearing a long woolen dress and a peasant fur coat that she had bought at the market. She also dressed me in a winter coat. I was hot and it bothered me the entire way.

When we arrived at the church, a great crowd had already filled the entrance. Tall men wearing long shirts were standing against the walls. Inside, next to the coffin, were some old people, and behind them women were weeping. Halina had gone up to the sky and soon she would return to me. I told myself that if only they knew that, they wouldn't be crying, but I also couldn't hold back my tears.

When they brought the coffin in through the doorway of the church, the flutes burst into a brisk tune. "Halina is ascending to heaven," I called out in a whisper. Mother must have picked up what I whispered, and she reacted with an irritated gesture. Mother considers all faith meaningless, just superstition. She already said to me once, "There's no God in the sky, only clouds." She also warned Halina not to tell me religious tales. When she heard this, Halina chuckled, as if she were being instructed to do something quite impossible.

As we walked slowly behind the coffin, the gates of light in the sky opened up and a great brightness poured down on us. The people bowed their heads so as not to see Halina rising to heaven. I wasn't afraid because I knew that she would return to me soon.

The skies closed and we didn't approach the grave. The priest spoke, and the village elder, too. They talked about Halina's youth and her love of life, and reviled the murderer. I was happy that I understood Halina's language.

After the funeral they declared that there would be a feast. Mother and I did not join the mourners but returned to the carriage awaiting us. There was no doubt now that Halina was making her way toward me, and out of sheer foolishness I told this to Mother. Mother looked at me and said, "There is no life after death. We have to get this fact into our heads." There was tremendous impatience in her voice.

"Halina told me that Jesus rose after His crucifixion," I insisted for some reason.

"It's a legend."

"And a legend is always a lie?"

"On the whole."

Mother does not believe in God; she had told me this on one of our outings during the summer vacation. How could you not believe in God, when He's there in every single place? Even the trees and the flowers thank Him every morning. On that vacation I was so happy to be by the water and to be so close to Mother that I didn't bother her with lots of questions. To tell the truth, I didn't care. But since meeting Halina, I know for sure that there's a God and that He's watching over us, that He loves those who are good and hates and punishes the wicked.

Halina told me that the new Jews do not believe in God and so they are in constant danger. Mother of course does not like those who believe. And now, too, all the way to Storozynetz, she spoke harshly against the rabbis and priests, and didn't stop until she had said, "Those people darken the world with their primitive rituals."

My head was spinning from all this talk. So as to hold on to my faith, I kept repeating to myself that Halina only appeared outwardly to have died, that she was in hiding, and the day was near when she would reveal herself to me.

We returned home and didn't speak of Halina's death. Mother was concerned that she had not yet found a suitable woman to take care of me. This was a very real threat for me, but I was not afraid. I knew that Halina was faithful and that at the first opportunity she would come back to me.

That night I did not sleep at all. As soon as Mother had slipped out of the house, I got up and stood by the window. The darkness was thick, and I searched for the path behind the house; I was sure this was the way by which Halina would return. Toward morning I was certain that I saw a woman climbing over the gate, but I was mistaken. I opened the window and called, "Halina!" On hearing my shout, the woman fled. Mother returned in the morning and I pretended to be asleep.

In the meantime, to keep me busy Mother filled up a notebook with math problems. They weren't hard and I solved them in less than an hour. Mother came back, checked them, and declared, "Excellent!" I told myself that if she saw that I solved math problems and practiced my handwriting day in and day out, she'd give up on her search for a woman to look after me. I swore to myself that from then on if I saw Halina at night, I wouldn't call out her name, but I'd wait for her patiently.

28

The surprise came from where I least expected it. While I was wandering the streets and returning to places I had been with Halina—sad and happy by turns—I saw Father. He was so glad to see me that he immediately snatched me up, lifting me high. We went straight into a café.

I hadn't seen Father for a long time. I'd almost forgotten what he looked like, and only in dreams did I see him. I had asked Mother many times why he didn't visit me. Mother gave long, indirect answers, and I didn't understand a thing. Now he stood in front of me as I remembered him: very tall, a peaked cap on his head, and a thin, shy smile hovering about his lips.

I told him about the murder.

Father listened without asking questions. He did not ask and did not argue. Sometimes I thought that he didn't know how to share other people's sorrow. Of course this wasn't so. He was a man without words, and you had to gaze at his face and his hands to learn from them. It was from his trembling hands that I knew he'd been drinking a lot recently. His eyes were swollen, which meant that he had not been sleeping much.

After I finished my cocoa he told me that Mother was about to be married, and he was going to take me with him.

"And what will become of Halina?" I asked.

"It will be fine," he told me with a nice smile.

The rumor about Mother's marriage had reached him. It was hard to know if he was depressed or angry. When Father was angry his hands shook and he held his head to the side. On the way home, I wanted to ask him not to be angry, but I didn't dare. Mother was at home and let us in silently. Father immediately told her that he intended to take me with him to Czernowitz. Mother didn't ask why, as I had expected her to, but she said, "I'll get his clothes ready, and in a week everything will be clean and packed in a suitcase."

"I won't be able to come in a week," Father said without looking at her.

"I don't have a housekeeper, and all the clothes are dirty."

"It doesn't matter," he said, and he covered his mouth with his hand.

Mother must have been scared, for she immediately began to put my clothes into the green suitcase. Father stood there, looking at her without saying a word. He must have been angry. His anger now had a dark aspect. When she started to put in my toys, the dominos and the balls, she burst into tears. Father watched her crying without interfering. I went over to her and hugged her. Mother kissed me again and again, and her tears covered my face. Father muttered something and then swallowed his mumbling.

The suitcase was overflowing and would not close. Father got down on his knees, grasped it with his two hands, pressed on the lid, and latched it shut. He looked at me and said, "Let's go."

"Paul." Mother turned to me with a choked voice. "I'll come to see you in a few days." And immediately she added, "I've put the math book and the notebook for practicing handwriting in a folder."

"I'll do all the problems," I said, wanting to please her.

"See you soon," she said, and raised her right hand, as if she were about to take an oath.

I looked up at her; her face was swollen, stained with red blotches, as if she had fallen or been slapped. And so we left the house. Mother stood on the steps, and as we walked away I could feel her following us with her eyes, but I didn't turn to look at her. Father walked along with his large strides, and I stumbled after him.

I felt the sudden parting from Mother only at the snack counter in the railway station. It seemed that I had parted from her long ago, and that only now did I feel it. Father bought me a sandwich and a bottle of lemonade and sat next to me.

"Father," I said, trying to start a conversation.

"What?" Father's eyes widened.

"What will I do in Czernowitz?"

Father fixed his gaze on me, and I immediately felt that my question had made him uneasy.

The train was delayed, and Father lit cigarette after cigarette. At last, when it did come, people burst onto the platform and rushed for the doors. The conductors tried to stop the crowd, but the people were stronger than they were. It was not long before everyone was pressed inside.

29

The train moved slowly, stopping at the small stations and taking on many passengers at each one. I was tired and dozed most of the way. In my sleep some of the sights from Halina's funeral returned to me, and for a moment it seemed that Halina would be waiting at the station in Czernowitz, and that we should hurry to get to her. Father took several gulps from the flask in his pocket. His face lit up and he gazed at me. Whenever this happened I felt waves of warmth flowing out from within him.

One of the drunks on the train buttonholed Father and told him about his wife and his daughters, who he said were cheating on him and stealing his money. Father listened and asked some questions. The drunk then told him at great length how his wife was deceiving him, being unfaithful, and how his daughters had gone astray. "I'll kill them, you know. I really will. I'll kill them at the very first opportunity! True, you can be hung for a murder, but I'm not afraid."

Father passed him the flask, and the man took a long gulp and blessed him. Although I could speak only a bit of Ruthenian, I understood the language. It is a language that has the scent of a corn-flour pie filled with plums. When Halina spoke Ruthenian, her face lit up and she laughed.

Near Czernowitz, Father fell asleep. It had been a long time since I had seen him sleep. When he slept, the pain surfaced. For years he'd struggled with people who embittered his life, and although he was tall and strong, they seemed to get the better of him. People didn't hate Mother. Mother was full of charm and closer to people. There were two art critics in Czernowitz who were particularly unpleasant to Father. Once, on one of our walks, he had pointed them out to me. He had said, "Those two are murderers." They hadn't seemed like murderers to me, but like two people innocently taking a walk. I had asked Father about this. He had explained and explained it, and then I understood for the first time how hard it was for him to speak of it, and that I shouldn't make it harder with more questions.

Once, he had pointed them out to me in a café and said, "God is dead in their hearts." I had wanted to ask him about this but didn't. His face had been dark and his jaw clenched in anger.

Then Father awoke and asked, "You're not asleep? We'll be reaching Czernowitz in a little while, and we'll take a walk." He loved long walks. I often wandered around the streets and the banks of the Prut with him. On these walks, his anger would subside and his face would soften. Sometimes he would stop, shade his eyes, and stare for a long time. I liked it when he did this.

It was already dark when we reached Czernowitz. I remembered the railway station from the summer vacation with Mother. Now it was empty and neglected. Everyone was hurrying to leave, and so were we. At first it seemed that we were going to get on the tram, but then Father changed his mind and said, "Just one drink and then we'll carry on."

As soon as he was inside the tavern, he gulped down one drink and then another one, embraced the waitress, and gave her a kiss. In this dim hall, filled with tobacco smoke, cognac, and beer, Father's face lit up and he talked in full sentences. People questioned him, joked around, and stared at me. Father introduced me. "Paul is nine, and he's already learning algebra; he reads and writes German and understands French."

It was a spacious hall, filled with long trestle tables. Everyone was speaking Ruthenian, spiced with bits of Romanian and German. I understood only a few confused words. Father wanted to please me and took a bar of chocolate from his coat pocket. We sat there until I got dizzy and fell asleep.

When I awoke, I was already in Father's arms on the way to the tram. On the tram, Father ran into an acquaintance and told him that he had just arrived from Storozynetz and was on his way home. The man looked at me and chuckled. In his small eyes there was a malicious look that frightened me. Father is never afraid after a few drinks. I've noticed how he's a different person, alert and full of witty sayings that amuse people so much that they laugh till the tears run down their cheeks.

Father's house was one long room, with the toilet outside. He lived on the outskirts of the city in the home of a Ruthenian peasant. The room was full of books and was not tidy. There were even clothes and books piled on the windowsill. Father poured me a glass of milk and made me a sandwich. I saw how carefully his large hands held the round bread. He sat near me, and I felt that he wanted to tell me something. But I was wrong, of course. After an hour of ease, the gloom returned. When the gloominess descends on his face, he shrinks in an instant, and sits and stares.

"Father," I called.

"What?"

"Can I have another sandwich?" I knew that asking him would make him happy, and he immediately went to prepare it for me. After he gave me the sandwich, he opened a book and began studying it.

"Halina," I called in a whisper, "now that the murderer's been sent to the gallows, there's nothing to fear. You can come down to me. I'm in Father's room, and I feel very alone."

30

The next day, Father left for his high school and I stayed alone in the room. In the daylight, it looked narrow and sooty. I opened the window and my eyes widened: the huge river, the River Prut, flowed right outside the house. I was so delighted that from sheer happiness I ran outside. Halina had told me so much about the Prut. I hadn't imagined that it could be so powerful. I stood on the bank and didn't dare touch the water.

The landlord saw me and asked, "Who are you?"

I told him my name.

He looked at me, smiled, and said, "It's you." Father must have told him that I was coming.

The river was surging, its waves breaking against the banks. It was frighteningly wide, but I overcame my fear and stayed where I was. Once, Halina told me, "You mustn't be afraid." I try to do everything she told me.

I wrapped my coat around me and sat gazing at the flowing river. Father had left me sandwiches, fruit, and a small bar of chocolate. Whenever I got hungry, I went back to the room, nibbled at something, and returned to the river.

It's strange—yesterday I was in Storozynetz and here I

am today. Did Mother also see me, just as I saw her now? Mother taught in her school, and in the afternoons she went to André. At night they lay naked in bed, embracing and kissing. This thought came back to me again and again and drove me crazy. I tried to push it out of me.

Suddenly, I saw Mother standing as she stood when Father took me away with him, her face swollen and a cry of fear frozen on her lips. I immediately swore to myself that as soon as I grew up I would go and rescue her from that blond thug. This thought so stirred me that I left the Prut and went inside.

The light grew colder, and snowflakes drifted down in the wind and melted as they landed. Last night, with absolute clarity, I saw Halina borne aloft on the wings of angels. It was a peaceful, blue sight. When she saw me, she called out with a mischievous smile, "Why don't you visit me in the chapel? I'm there most of the day." I remembered her once telling me that, through prayer, we can change everything. If we are fated to die, prayer can cancel the decree.

"If prayer is so strong, why don't people pray?" I asked.

"They don't know its power; if they knew, they would pray." She spoke not only of prayer but of God as well. "If man believes in God, God dwells within him and no harm can befall him."

"I don't understand, Halina."

"Through prayer we are connected to Him; the trees and the birds are also connected to Him."

"God is everything," I said.

Halina was so amazed at what I said, she hugged me and kissed me and would not stop till she had said, "I'll gobble you all up and there'll be nothing left of you!"

It was always hard to guess what Father was thinking. Sometimes it seemed that he talked only with God, but there were days when I sensed that he was not connected to anyone, not even to God, and that he lived by himself, all alone, and no one knew his secret.

And so I sat and gazed at the waters of the Prut, and it occurred to me that if everything was connected to God, the Prut was also connected to Him, so there was nothing to fear from it.

In the afternoon, it rained. I had hoped that when the rain stopped I could stand on the riverbank, but it rained harder and I got drenched. I went inside, stood next to the window, and saw battalions of clouds racing through the skies and lashing their rain down on the black waters of the Prut. It was a struggle between heaven and earth, and it was hard to understand what it was about. So I sat and observed. And the longer I sat, the more I saw everything darkening; it was clear to me that Halina would not visit me here. My prayers at night returned empty. I opened the door and went outside. The rain and the wind whipped my face, and I felt a pressure in my chest. "God, let me see Halina!" I called out.

"She's in the chapel" came the answer. "If you come to Storozynetz, you'll be able to see her. Many people come to see her."

31

Father returns when it's dark. I am so happy that I forget my woes. Father is also happy. When Father's happy his forehead gets broader and the lines on it rise.

Father gets up to make a pot of potatoes for dinner. He buys provisions from our landlord. The landlord brings the provisions and hastens to extol their quality and freshness. Father tries to make this conversation as brief as possible, but the landlord goes on and on. He talks about the rains and crop yields, and the flooding that has uprooted an entire orchard. Father pays him and promises that he'll come and see the new plot of land he's bought. The landlord leaves, and we sit at the table to eat our meal: baked potatoes, cheese, and yogurt.

Father doesn't ask, "How was it?" or "What did you do?" He eats and then serves up more for me and for himself. It appears as though this is his only full meal of the day. To break the silence, I tell him how I sat on the riverbank and gazed at the water. I would have really liked him to ask me about Storozynetz and about Halina, but he does not ask, as if he has no curiosity. And yet his presence does not weigh heavily on me. I love to have him close to me, so sturdy, and I think that one day I'll be like him.

When it stops raining, we go into town. Once our walks were less leisurely; now we stroll about the alleyways and walk up the main streets. The downtown area is crowded at night, with the stores and cafés open. At the café, Father knows many people, and they greet him cheerfully. In the street, too, he meets acquaintances. Sometimes it seems to me that the entire city likes him, and I'm proud of him.

It's not always like that. Once, a short, stocky man approached us, and I saw that Father became filled with anger. The man was an art critic, as it turned out, one of Father's enemies. Although I knew that he doesn't usually beat up people, I was still afraid. But this time Father surprised me and called out, "You scum! I hope the worms will eat you!" The man must have heard the curse; he began to run toward the gate of a house and then disappeared inside. Father's fury abated and a cold smile spread over his face.

Our walks usually wind up at the tavern. Father downs a couple of drinks, jokes with the barmaid, asks after his friends, and then we return home. I fall asleep on the tram, and Father carries me home in his arms. When I wake up in the morning, I feel as though I'm still sitting in the café.

The rains do not cease, and most of the day I sit by the window and gaze at the Prut flowing by. The river is black, and its waters surge and break over the banks with a deafening noise. Sometimes the landlord comes in and asks how I'm doing. Once, he asked me if I went to synagogue. I was taken aback by his question, and I told him the truth. "A person should go to pray at least once a week so that he'll remember that there's a God in the world," he said. "The new Jews never go to see the face of God in the synagogue as they're commanded. The café is their temple. God has been showing restraint, but not for long. When the time comes,

He'll punish them." His face was red, and he spoke in a voice that shocked me.

"I'll go to the synagogue," I said, very frightened.

"Every Sabbath, like your forefathers used to go. You promise?"

"I'll try."

"That's not enough."

"I promise."

"Say 'I promise and I will keep to it,'" he said, and a broad smile spread over his ruddy face.

At this time of the year the landlord does not work in the fields, only in the cowshed and the chicken coop. But like me, he sits at the window for hours, gazing at the River Prut. On Sundays he puts on a suit and goes to church. He leaves quietly, circumspectly. But when he comes back from church in the afternoon, his face is red and he's singing hymns.

Once I heard him talking to his neighbor, a peasant like himself, and this is what he said: "People have forgotten that there's a God in the world, and they think that everything's up for grabs. There *is* order and a purpose in the world. Whoever does not see this is blind or dumb—but how can I talk? Even my own sons have gone astray. If a man does not respect his father, he ends up not respecting our Father in heaven. His own father does not have it within his power to punish him, but God is wise and mighty, and He'll bring him to a reckoning."

32

When Father returned home, I told him about the land-lord's visit. Father laughed and said, "Don't take any notice of him. In the winter he's drunk and talks only about God. But he's a good man."

"Is there a God in the sky?" I could not contain myself.

"There is, apparently," said Father, and chuckled, as if someone had discovered his weakness.

Then he reconsidered and said, "Why did you ask?"

I told him about Halina and how she rose to heaven. His forehead creased all at once, and he said, "The Rutheni-ans still have a simple faith, and we should learn from them."

It wasn't raining, so Father decided that in the evening we would go to the church refectory and celebrate, and so we did. I loved the city streets at night after the rain. Nights such as those become absorbed deep inside you, and you remember them for a long time. Once, on a night after it had rained, I went with Father to Herrengasse, where he met an old friend. They stood talking, and before they parted, the man said, "I don't know what to do; I feel lost." The man and the words that had come out of his mouth seemed to me so inseparable, as if they were one, that now, whenever it stops raining and I'm in the street, I see that man and hear his voice.

The refectory was full of heavy wooden tables and somewhat resembled a tavern, except that here people drank only lemonade. There were just a few drunks, and they didn't disturb anyone. Father got two pieces of corn pie at the counter, a jug of cream, and two glasses of lemonade. We immediately found seats by the window.

The hall was completely filled, and it was hard to speak. If you looked up, you saw that the walls and the ceiling were covered with pictures of saints. A large metal light fixture hung from the ceiling. The place didn't look like a church, and yet it bore some resemblance. The corn pie was tasty, and Father hurried to fetch more. All the while, people came up to him, asking how he was. I noticed that here, too, everyone was slapping him on the shoulder and calling him by his first name. Father had had his hair cut a few days earlier, and he looked like a soldier just out of the army.

After we finished the meal, the people buried their faces in their hands and started to sing. It was a restrained but powerful singing that seemed as if it would flow that way for hours, except suddenly the door at the back opened and a very thin, very elderly man came in and those singing fell silent.

As the old man sat on a chair, all eyes were on him.

"Dear brothers," he began, "may the light of the Messiah be upon you and may your eyes see only the light and only the good. Do not quarrel among yourselves, for such dissention comes from darkness and from Satan. Beloved brothers, do not fight, for fighting removes us from His light and expels us into darkness."

The old man was dressed in peasant's clothing and

spoke Ruthenian. A harsh light radiated from his long, gaunt face. I did not understand most of what he said, but I knew that he was talking about God and about the light and about people who are drawn to the darkness and refuse to see the light. He also spoke of Jews who deny the Messiah and have gone astray and lead others astray. There was great stillness, and the voice of the old man carried through the hall like a frightening threat. But apparently people were not afraid—they sat alertly, as if the old man was about to lead them into a world filled with goodness.

When the old man had finished, two strong men went up to him, supported his forearms, and helped him to the doorway at the back. No one rose from his seat; it was as if everyone had stopped breathing. For a long time the silence hung in the air until a peasant stood up and called out, "There is none like our God and there is none like our Messiah!" and immediately the hall burst into mighty song.

Once Halina had taken me to a church and shown me the altar. It was a small, wooden church with angels on its windows. The priest was wearing his ceremonial robes and reading from a big book, and the choir began to sing whenever he finished a section. I do not know whether this was a festival or a funeral, but in any case, then, too, the priest had called out, "There is none like our God and there is none like our Messiah!"

We went outside and Father lit a cigarette. The night was dark and the gates of heaven, which only a moment ago had seemed open, suddenly closed.

We crossed the street and waited at the tram station. There was no one there. I wanted to ask Father why the heavens were sealed off and for how long they would be sealed off, but his head was buried so deep in the collar of his coat that I didn't dare. The tram was not long in coming, and we sat in the front seat, as if we were about to set out on a long journey to a place where the heavens are always open and you can see God clearly, sitting on His throne.

33

The rain grew fiercer each day, and hail fell in the evening. Father would come back in the dark and immediately start to make dinner. The dampness that he brought with him from outside mingled with the scent of the wood burning in the stove. We mostly ate potatoes, cheese, and yogurt, but sometimes Father brought corn pie from the city and we dipped it in sour cream. When he was in a good mood, he would show me drawings his students made.

"Very nice," I said—an expression that Mother often uses.

"Where did you get that shallow expression?" Father wondered.

"Was I wrong?"

"'Very nice' is not a nice expression," Father said, and chuckled.

My life at Storozynetz was forgotten, and Mother, too. When we walked around in the city, I sometimes thought I saw Halina. Once I pulled my hand away from Father and ran to a woman who looked like her. Her memory evoked sunlight for me, and I told myself that in summer she would return and we'd walk along the river. After our meal, Father sat and looked at a book, and I leafed through one of his many art volumes. The children's books that I'd brought with me from Storozynetz no longer interested me. I felt that the stories and pictures in them had died, and reading them wouldn't bring them back to life. Under a picture in one of Father's books I read the word "portrait," and I asked Father what it meant. Father looked at me with a level gaze, and for the first time I saw two lines etched the length of his face. I sensed the hidden fury in them and I was scared.

"Why are you scared?"

"I'm not scared." I tried to deny it.

This time Father stood his ground. "You have to be strong and you mustn't be afraid. Fear is indecent. A man has to uproot it from his heart." I marveled at these full sentences coming from him—he usually spoke in words and not in sentences.

Sometimes Father raised his head from his book and asked me something. It was hard for me to explain to him what I felt or thought. Since Halina had left me, it was hard for me to talk. With Halina I would chatter, joke, and even invent words that would make her laugh. Now I found it hard to put a sentence together.

Most of the daylight hours I was at home alone, and when the rain let up, I would go out and stand on the riverbank. The landlord came again and asked me about praying. It was hard for me to lie to him, and I said, "No." A sad smile appeared on his lips, and he told me that years ago, Jews who believed lived in these parts. They would pray every day, to say nothing of Sabbaths and other festivals.

"And where are they?"

"They've scattered."

"Why?"

"Who knows?"

"And there are no more Jews who believe?"

"There are, but fewer and fewer."

Strange, it was easier for me to talk with this Ruthenian peasant than with Father. The landlord told me about the Jews in the countryside who used to till their land like the Ruthenians, keeping God's commandments, not working on the Sabbath, and giving to the needy. He seemed to miss them.

"Is it good to be a Jew?" I asked for some reason.

"It's a great privilege, my son. God spoke to the Jews at Mount Sinai and gave them the Torah. Since then the entire world knows that there is a God in heaven and that the world isn't up for grabs. You see?"

"So why did they throw stones at me and call me a dirty Jew?"

"They're afraid of you."

"Why are they afraid of me?"

"Because you're the son of a king."

"Me?"

"You."

It was hard for me to really comprehend his words, and I asked, "Why am I the son of a king?"

"Because God spoke to your forefathers and adopted you as his son."

"I'm only nine years old."

"You're a little prince, and when you get bigger, you'll be a prince." Then he added in a sad tone, "The Jews no longer know who they are. Once they knew, but now they've forgotten and we have to remind them. Do you understand me?"

"A little."

"They've forgotten that they're the sons of kings."

I asked Father about what the landlord said. Father was brief as usual and said, "He's a man who believes."

"And we don't believe?"

"Not to that extent."

Mother explained; Father never explained. He hated explanations. Once, when were sitting in a tavern, I asked him why he didn't explain, to which he responded, "If you understand, you understand; explanations are useless."

34

One morning the door opened and there stood Mother. She had cut her hair and was wearing a long, heavy coat. I almost didn't recognize her. "It's me, my dear," she said, and I went over to her. She tried to pick me up, but her heavy sleeves got in the way, and for a moment she stayed bent over my neck, embarrassed by her failure. But then she immediately took my face in her hands and kissed it.

"How are you?" she asked, taking off her coat. A little of the strangeness left her, and I saw then how her face had filled out and her hair had faded.

"You're alone?"

"Yes."

"Where's Father?"

"At work."

"Strange," she said, as if only now had she grasped that she was there.

"Why strange?"

"I don't know."

She stood there, looking around the room. It was a mess, and she didn't like the soot. She put her hand to her forehead, a gesture that I remembered well, a gesture of dissatisfaction and sometimes despair.

"Come, I'll show you the Prut." I tried to extricate her from her confusion.

"But it's raining."

"We'll put our coats on."

Reluctantly, she put on her coat and we went out.

The Prut was now a dark brown; it cast its heavy waves against the bank. This was my mother, and yet she was so different. The heavy coat made her look shorter, and her long arms seemed truncated. We stood and watched for a short time. There was no beauty in the sight. The wet wind lashed at our faces. "Let's go inside, otherwise we'll be soaked to the bone," she said. She was wearing rural galoshes that made her legs look thicker.

We sat at the table, and Mother took out the gifts she had brought in her bag: a particularly large set of dominos, a pack of cards, and, best of all, Suchard chocolate.

"How do you spend all your time, my dear?"

"I read."

"What do you read?"

"Father's books." I tried to impress her.

"They're very hard books," she said, as if she had caught me attempting something that was beyond me. To tell the truth, I didn't like her inflection.

"You've changed." The words just slipped from my mouth.

"In what way?"

"I don't know."

Mother took some sandwiches out of her bag and then immediately removed them from the wax paper in which they had been wrapped. I remembered Mother's sandwiches. That's how she used to prepare them in our home in Czernowitz, and after that in Storozynetz. There was something of her grace in them. I immediately bit into one.

"I've come to fetch you," she said.

"To where?"

"To Storozynetz."

"No," I wanted to say but stopped myself.

Mother must have sensed my refusal, for she said, "I've found a nice girl, like Halina."

"And Halina isn't coming?" I interrupted her.

"What are you talking about, my dear?"

"I'm sorry."

She said nothing about André or the wedding. There was no need to say anything; the expression on her face said it—that she was now married to André, preparing meals for him, washing his shirts, and laughing with him. But her face was not happy. It was somewhat frozen, and the more I stared at it, the more frozen it seemed, as if the tiny veins of happiness had been drained from it. She was the mother that I had once loved, and yet not. We sat without talking.

"We'll pack your clothes and go back home," she said in a whisper.

"I don't want to go," I replied in a clear voice.

My words must have astonished her; she put her right hand to her mouth and her eyes lost their luster.

"I love the river." I tried to soften it.

"And you don't want to come with me?"

"Not now."

"I understand," she said, and her eyes moved slightly.

Then she put on her coat and closed her bag. She didn't try to convince me, not even by so much as a word. I knew that I was being cruel to her, but I also knew what I wanted, and nothing in me stirred toward her.

"I won't force you," she said as she buttoned her coat. She must have expected me to waver, but I didn't.

The falling rain struck the door and the windows, darkening the room. "It's raining," I said, trying to keep her from going.

"Never mind," she said, lifting her collar. She kissed my forehead and went out.

I stood in the doorway and watched her grow distant. She made her way heavily, as if leaving a place she found distasteful.

"Mother!" I called, but my voice couldn't have reached her. I kept calling, my voice choking. I put on my coat and ran after her, but the rain and the mud dragged me down and I turned back. I sat at the window and waited for her to return. It was clear that she wouldn't, but with my thoughts I still tried to will her back to me.

35

Throughout the long hours of the afternoon I sat at the window, waiting for Mother to return. When it got dark, I heard footsteps approaching; it was Father. Father came back in good spirits. He had had a few drinks on the way home, and the moment he walked in, he announced, "Dinner should be lavish." I was happy, too, and forgot to tell him about Mother's visit. I told him later.

"And what did she want?" he asked lightly.

"To take me back with her."

"I understand. And what did you say?"

"I refused."

"And what did she say?"

"Nothing."

Father did not scold me, and he did not praise my behavior. We sat up till late, he on the bed and I on the floor. Father read intently and I watched, observing how his eyes raced from line to line. When he read, he looked like a man who is searching. Sometimes he seemed to be searching for something he lost many years ago. I noticed that when he finished reading, he made a gesture of dismissal with his right hand, as if to say, "It's all nonsense."

That night he revealed to me that Mother had married

and was living in André's house. It was hard to know if he was angry. Whenever he spoke about Mother, he was careful, and it was clear he did not reveal all his thoughts to me.

"Has she become Christian?" I asked for some reason.

"Supposedly," he said.

"But we are Jews, aren't we?"

"True."

Then I remembered what our landlord had said, and my heart was sore. I tried to remember it in detail, but I couldn't. Later, I recalled a bit and asked, "Is it true that Jews are the sons of kings?"

"Who told you that?" Father laughed quietly.

"The landlord."

"He lives in a world of his own."

"Jews are like everyone else?"

"A little less," Father said, and chuckled again.

I was indignant that Mother had converted. "Why did she convert?" I asked.

"Because she married André."

Later, I could see her before me: her cropped hair, her legs in their heavy galoshes, and the difficulty she had in walking. The expression on her face was that of a person whose thoughts had been uprooted, with other thoughts implanted in their place. We talked no more that night. Father read and I leafed through his art books. I didn't understand most of the things that I read in Father's books, but I still liked to go through them. Sometimes I wanted to ask him the meaning of a word, but I didn't. Once, he blamed me for interrupting his reading.

One morning when I was looking through his books I saw Father's name and I gasped. I read it again: *Arthur Rosenfeld*. On the facing page there was a photo of him when he was young. Father, it turned out, was born in Czernowitz in

1905. His parents died when he was five years old, and he grew up in an orphanage. It was at the orphanage that his talent was recognized, and he was sent to study at the Academy for Fine Arts. When he was fifteen, there was an exhibition of his work at the celebrated Leonardo da Vinci Gallery; the exhibition traveled to Vienna and then on to Salzburg. Two years later, he exhibited at the Cézanne Gallery, then back in Czernowitz, and then on to Vienna and other major cities. "A remarkable artist whose marvels we'll likely see more of in the future," ran a line from that paragraph. I read it again and again, unable to believe my eyes.

In the evening Father returned tired and depressed, his face dark and somber. It was clear that he had had several drinks, but they didn't relieve his depression. When Father was depressed his face became taut and his jaw clenched; the sockets of his eyes darkened and his eyes seemed to sink into them. He prepared our evening meal without uttering a word.

36

I sit at home looking through a book on the history of art. The word "expressionism" crops up on almost every page. It's as if it's a magic word, and if I knew how to pronounce it, I'd be enlightened, and wiser. Two of Father's drawings are in the book. In the first you can make out utensils and fruit, and in the second, a young woman wearing a wide-brimmed straw hat. The woman looks like Mother, not the Mother who was here some days ago, but the Mother who was with me over the summer vacation by the tributary of the Prut.

Now I can picture Father as a beloved prince borne aloft on his admirers' shoulders, greeted in every city with flowers. Father does not speak, as the way of princes is not to speak. But now there is no one who knows that Father is a prince. In the city he has many acquaintances, but they also don't know that he is a prince. They speak to him as an equal. If they only knew, they would kneel before him. Our landlord has worked out a bit of the secret. Once he said to me, "Your father is a real prince; it's a pity that he doesn't pray." I showed the landlord the book, and I pointed to Father's name and to his two paintings.

"I didn't know that he was a painter, but I knew he was a real prince," he told me.

"How can you tell?"

"By his features. There are many real princes among the Jews, but they've forgotten who they are and they behave like anyone else."

"Why have they forgotten?"

"It must be God's will."

"And when will they wake up from their forgetting?"

"Who knows?"

At this time of the year the landlord works in the yard. When it rains he's in the cowshed or the barn. He walks slowly, mumbling to himself. Sometimes he speaks to the animals as if to partners who labor alongside him. Once I saw a cow giving birth to a calf. I could not bear the sight of the blood and the pain, and I went into the house.

I want to ask Father about the days when he would paint and travel with his paintings from city to city. But I don't ask because I know there are secrets of which one must not speak. Father guards a big secret; if you get too near to his secret, his face darkens.

Once, he saw me looking through the book about the history of art and said, "That's not for you." I kept quiet and did not tell him that I had discovered his secret. "Why don't you read your own books?"

"They don't interest me." I didn't hide it from him.

A smile spread over his face, and I knew that he understood me.

At night we go to the church refectory. It is full, and they serve corn pie, with milk and cream, at the counters. Father meets many acquaintances here, and they slap him on the shoulder. They say that the old man is sick and that it is doubtful that he will preach. It's a shame that here they don't know that Father is a prince. If they knew, they would carry him like they carry the venerable old man. True, Father is a silent prince, and he guards his secret behind seven doors. If he would only let me bring along that book, *The History of Art in the Austro-Hungarian Empire,* and show them the photo of Father and his two pictures, then they would believe me. They would cheer and crown him.

This evening the old man does not speak, but everyone sings. It is a thunderous song that shakes the walls of the hall. People cover their faces with their hands, and Father also sings with his eyes closed.

Then we walk for hours in the fine rain, visiting churches and galleries. Father does not like the pictures in the galleries, and he is particularly angry with a gallery that shows Jews in traditional clothes, calling it a desecration of man and other names that I don't understand. Before we take the tram, we go into a tavern and Father downs a drink or two. In the tram he suddenly says to me, "There are things that we will never understand."

I know his mind is elsewhere, and yet I still feel that he is offering me a fragment of his mystery.

37

Cold, gray days follow and the sun is nowhere to be seen. Snow falls darkly and incessantly, covering the roofs and the fences. Even the mighty Prut stops roaring. Father comes home drunk and depressed and throws himself onto the bed. I don't know what to do, so I just sit next to him. When his depression worsens, he tears up papers and drawings, tossing them into the mouth of the furnace. This is no longer anger, but despair. The work at his school leaves him totally exhausted, the students have no talent, and the administration drains his vitality. "What am I asking, after all—just a little time and a studio!" he bursts out, and it seems to me that blood will spurt from his mouth, and I am shocked, frightened.

Every morning, while it's still dark, Father dresses and leaves to catch the first tram. His departure freezes the darkness of the room, and it seeps into me throughout the day. Sometimes I feel that I must be a burden to him and I want to slip away. When I told him that, he began to cry. Now he occasionally cries, and it's more frightening than his anger.

The landlord comes in every evening, bringing us provisions. Father scarcely talks to him and asks nothing. The landlord doesn't take offense. "Arthur, my dear, you mustn't despair, there is a God in heaven," he says. Father raises his eyes as if to say, "Why should you torture me, too?" The landlord lowers his head, mutters a short blessing, and goes out.

But to me the landlord says something that shakes me: "God has removed Himself from him, and until he returns to his forefathers, he'll be tormented by demons. Where there is no God, there are demons; they breed like insects."

"What should one do?"

"Pray."

There is a kind of certainty in his voice that shocks me.

I don't remember how long this darkness lasts. With every passing day Father's face darkens, and the trembling of his hands increases. I want to help him, but I don't know how. One evening he returns home drunk and happy, a telegram in his hand. A distant friend—a forgotten friend who lives in Bucharest and was once a gallery owner—writes that he is putting a house at Father's disposal and has prepared a generous advance for him. The telegram ends: COME TO US AT ONCE; THOSE WHO LOVE YOU AWAIT YOU. Father reads it and tears roll down his cheeks. The good news affects him so that he can hardly stand on his feet. We drink coffee and do not eat supper. Father calls Victor a savior from heaven. He swings me high, up to the ceiling, proclaiming jubilantly, "Bucharest! Who would have imagined that redemption would come from Bucharest?!" After this he says no more, and I see tiredness overcome him. He sleeps deeply, and his breathing is regular. I cover him with a blanket and am glad that God has hastened to his aid.

Snow falls, and from day to day it grows colder. The Prut changes color, and now it is a dark blue, a hard and unpleasant color.

I sit at home and look at books. Once a day the landlord comes to the door and gives me a pear or an apple. Father tells me that at the end of the month we will be on our way.

"Don't forget that you're Jewish," the landlord tells me when he comes back from the church, smelling of incense and in high spirits.

"I'll remember," I say, so as to make him happy.

"Jews tend to forget it."

In the evening we usually go downtown; we sit in a café or go into a tavern. Father is full of energy. He tells his acquaintances about his friend from way back who has invited him to Bucharest. Everyone's happy for him, joking around and wishing him inspiration for his work.

One evening he is set upon by a drunk, who calls him a dirty Jew. Father demands that the drunk apologize, but the man continues to curse him. Father hits him across the face, and the drunk collapses on the floor. Immediately, other drunks gather around, threatening Father. Father is quick to push them away, striking out fearlessly. I am afraid. On the way home he tells me, "You mustn't let wicked people get cocky; you have to beat them." It has been a long time since he's spoken in full, clear sentences. After that he calms down and is happy, telling me of his plans and about Bucharest, a gracious city with many galleries—a gateway to France. I'm wary of his enthusiasm. After he becomes enthusiastic, depression engulfs him.

The landlord takes care of us, and every evening he brings us one of the dishes he's prepared. Last night he brought us goat cheese. Father promises to write him a letter from Bucharest. I've noticed that with Father he doesn't talk about the things that he discusses with me—with Father he talks mainly about fields, crops, his neighbors, and how they're all being taxed. However, this time he allows himself to ask, "What are you going to do in the big city?"

"I'll paint."

"May God guide what you do," he says, and extends his hand.

Father bows his head, surprised at the blessing that the landlord bestowed on him.

Father packs up his books and sketchbooks and gives away the household utensils to people he knows. The landlord mutters angrily, "You're too generous. A man has to hang on to what he has," and he refuses to accept the big grandfather clock. Father persuades him by saying, "It's a loan, not a gift. The day will come when I'll take it back." The landlord consents, but not without reminding Father of the well-known proverb, Whoever hates gifts will live.

This packing up saddens me and reminds me of how Mother had packed. In just a few days we will be on our way, and I assume I won't see Mother anymore. Many of her expressions have already fled from my mind. Now I recall only what she looked like most recently, and the heavy coat she was wearing. I am sad that she has changed so much.

We go downtown every evening. It is cold and dry. The snow squeaks underfoot, and heavy shadows cling to the fences of the municipal park. I dress warmly. Father has bought me a pair of leather boots, a scarf, and a fur hat. "Bucharest is cold in winter, and we must have warm clothes," Father says, as if he has bought them for himself as well. One of Father's admirers, a tall woman in a luxurious fur coat, sidles up to him in the café and says, "In what way have we insulted you that you should leave us and set out for Bucharest?"

"Bucharest, apparently, understands the soul of an artist better than Czernowitz." Father speaks in a tone that I have never heard him use.

"We love him passionately—and we won't relinquish him so easily."

Father draws himself up, lifts her hand, and kisses it. He opens his heart and says, "Don't worry, I won't forget Czernowitz; this city is planted deep within my heart, and it will go with me wherever I go. A birthplace cannot be uprooted from the heart—even one that has been hard on you."

"Thank you," says the woman. Without raising her head from her collar, she turns and leaves. Father stands where he is and follows her with his eyes.

"Strange," says Father. We leave the café and go into a tavern. There he downs several drinks, and I must have fallen asleep, for the following morning I find myself in bed, as if I have been tossed up from the stormy waters of the Prut.

38

The next morning the landlord took four crates of books to the railway station in his wagon. The crates were to travel via the freight train while we followed them on the night train. I felt sad about the room that we were going to abandon. Father was shoving sketches and paintings into the blazing fire. The landlord tried to prevent this destructiveness but couldn't. Father was adamant: the flames alone could correct them.

In the evening the landlord brought us to the railway station. Father embraced him, saying, "You've been a brother and a true friend to us."

"May God bless you."

The landlord turned to me. "Don't forget what I told you."

"I won't forget," I promised.

"May God bless you both and keep you," he said. "You deserve it." He bowed and climbed back up onto the wagon.

And so we parted from the landlord. We still had another two and a half hours till the train would leave. Father was in a good mood. He bought me an ice cream and called the city a province that fattens up its rich. His enthusiasm does not usually last very long, an hour at the most, and sometimes even less, but this time I saw that he was comfortable with the parting. His eyes shone, and the dark rings around them had faded. A man called out to him. It was an old Jew who had once worked in the orphanage and recognized him. Father was glad to see him and invited him for a drink. The Jew refused. We sat at the station entrance, and Father told him that he was now leaving for Bucharest, where a spacious house and studio awaited him. The Jew listened with his head bent and didn't look excited. Finally he asked, "And a living?"

"Absolutely!" Father answered confidently.

They spoke of what had become of the boys from the orphanage — those who had remained in the city and those who had traveled far. The old man could recall all their names, and for a moment he looked at us intently, as if trying to fathom what awaited us far off. His gaze must have frightened Father, who immediately flooded him with talk, as if trying to deflect him. The old man understood that he had made a mistake and lowered his eyes. He stood silently, as if wishing to get away. To our surprise he then stretched out his hands and blessed us. First Father, and then me. Father was embarrassed and his face became flushed.

We entered a tavern. In the tavern Father met some poor acquaintances and ordered sandwiches and drinks for them. At the same time he told them that in another hour and a half we would be on the night train to Bucharest.

"Why are you going?" one spoke up.

"Because here all everyone cares about is money and there's no compassion in their hearts. The artists can starve."

"And in Bucharest?"

"In Bucharest artists get support and they can work."

"And won't you miss the city where you were born?"

"No."

"Strange."

"Not strange at all. No one has offered me a studio here, or an advance. I teach forty-six hours a week, and when I get home my hands are shaking from tiredness."

"They shake from the drink and not from tiredness."

"You shut up!" Father raised his voice.

"I'm speaking the truth. Jews have no respect for their city, for their birthplace. They're ready to go anywhere that will offer them more. A birthplace isn't a shop where you go in, buy something, and leave!"

"I'm leaving it gladly—and you, too."

"Now you know why Jews are hated."

Father did not hold himself back but got up and hit the man in the face. For his part, the man did not sit idly by with his hands in his pockets. "The Jews are worms!" he shouted.

"But not pigs!" shouted Father, and went on hitting him.

Those around them tried to separate the two brawlers, but Father was furious, cursing in every language he knew. He wouldn't let anyone near him. Eventually someone came and threw him outside. Father's face was covered in blood, and he tried to wipe it off with his handkerchief. The blood was spurting out, staining his shirt and pants, but Father looked far from wretched. A kind of fire flamed in his face. He cursed the town and its people and shouted, "I'll get you! You just wait, you bastards!"

At the station we found a faucet and Father washed his face. He took a shirt out of the suitcase, and turning toward the tavern, he shouted, "I'm not through with you!" Then we immediately got onto the train.

39

The train speeds along, not stopping at small stations. At night, the stations look like dimly lit warehouses. Bags and people are all mixed together, and small children jump around on the platforms and screech at the approaching trains. Father is tired and falls into a deep sleep.

I remember Mother. It's been many days since I've seen her face. Now I feel that I didn't behave well toward her. When she stood in the rain and said to me, "Farewell, my love," I stood staring at her as if it didn't affect me. I hadn't even walked with her as far as the tram, and now we were about to treat her shabbily, disappearing on her. She would certainly return here someday, dressed in the same heavy coat and clumsy galoshes, and she would look for us, and the landlord would say, "They've gone to Bucharest . . . they didn't leave an address." Mother would stand there as if in shock. She would try to put together a few words and would repeat the question, and the landlord would give her the same answer.

Halina once told me that God tests us all the time, like He did with Abraham. He tests children with small trials and grown-ups with more difficult ones. At that time I didn't understand what she was talking about. Now, I understand: God also tested me and I failed the test. When the time comes, I'll surely be punished because I didn't keep to what Halina used to drum into me morning and night: honoring one's mother is more important than honoring one's father. Because I didn't honor my mother, everyone insulted her. Whenever an insult landed on her, she would bury her head in the collar of her heavy coat.

"Mother, we'll see each other soon," I say with my last ounce of strength, and then I fall asleep.

When I awaken, the blood-red dawn is already outside the window. My head is resting against Father's side. He tells me that we are very near Bucharest and that in Bucharest we will eat breakfast. I try to picture the railway station in Bucharest. I imagine it to be like the station at Czernowitz, but I know that my imagination is playing tricks on me.

"Father," I say.

"What?"

I hope that Father will now tell me something about Bucharest, but he says nothing. His face is tense. I know why: he hasn't had a drink since last evening.

There isn't a soul waiting for us at the station. Victor, who has promised to come, has not. We stand by the exit and wait. The station at Bucharest is not at all like the station at Czernowitz. It's much grander, humming with people, and there are many policemen watching over those coming and going. We stand there with our suitcases, at the threshold of a strange city, like poor people who don't have a roof over their heads. Father lights one cigarette after another, and despair burns in his bloodshot eyes. Suddenly I see a bald man waving his hat, treading heavily in the gray morning mist. He looks like a drunk who has just woken up from a stupor, but we are wrong, for he turns out to be none other than Victor. Father runs toward him and hugs him.

Victor is a small, rotund man. He speaks German with a heavy accent, and after every few sentences he says, "It'll be fine; there's nothing to worry about." He invites us to a restaurant, and the breakfast is good. I particularly like the poppy seed rolls, which remind me of the vacation with Mother.

"Arthur," says Victor, and slaps Father's shoulder. It is obvious that he is happy to see him, and he expresses his happiness with his hands, by rubbing them together. He uses small expressions of encouragement and mentions the names of critics who once praised Father's paintings. For years Victor has dreamed of bringing Father to Bucharest, but he did not have enough money. Some six months ago, he came into an inheritance; his aunt left him her house and jewelry. "And now I can realize my old dreams. Come, let's go home."

"Is it far?" wonders Father.

"Five kilometers, possibly less."

"What I urgently need is a drink." Father speaks in a low voice.

"Right away," says Victor, and orders the waiter to bring one.

We take the tram and are on our way. We pass gray fields that are covered with dirty splotches of snow, frozen puddles, and low houses with thin wisps of smoke rising from their chimneys. Here and there is an abandoned house or a small factory. The fear that no one would meet us at the railway station and that we would wander around lost in a big city was groundless.

In the meantime, Victor reveals some of his plans: an exhibition in Bucharest and an exhibition in Paris. People are looking forward to it; the outlook is bright. The words roll rapidly from his mouth, and it's obvious that his inheritance has turned his head. Father does not ask any questions, which appears to increase the flow of words from Victor, as if he is trying to remove any doubt.

After half an hour's journey we arrive at the house, an impressive two-story mansion surrounded by a forest. Victor's aunt, his mother's sister, who left him the house, was a childless widow. She lived there all alone, devoted to the memory of her husband, whom she had loved with all her heart.

"And who was her husband?"

"A retired general. After finishing his service he converted to Judaism, learned Hebrew and Yiddish, and founded the Association for the War Against Anti-Semitism."

"Did it have many members?"

"A one-man association!" Victor says, laughing.

The house is spacious and filled with light, the ceilings are high, and the floors are made of fine wood. Victor embraces Father. "The time has come for artists to create in ease and comfort. Poverty is humiliating."

I recall our room in Czernowitz, and I know what he is talking about.

40

And so our life has suddenly changed. Father works in his studio every day, and I drift about the house. It's full of rooms. I go from one to another and end up sitting in the kitchen, solving math problems that I make up and doodling. Victor has brought me two pads, one for math and one for drawing, and I sit and fill them. When I'm tired I go outside. It's very cold, and the trees are covered with snow. Unlike our room in Czernowitz, which was next to the Prut, here everything's quiet, and were it not for the crows hopping over the surface of the snow, one could hear the silence, as Mother says.

My life in Czernowitz now seems distant, hardly mine at all. Sometimes I feel as if the Ruthenian landlord is standing behind the house and will soon appear, saying, "The Jews have forgotten that they are Jews." I'm afraid of his words; there's always some unpleasant demand in them. I know that this is his drunkenness speaking, and yet I'm still afraid. At these moments I'm glad that we've left that narrow room and removed ourselves from the landlord and his religious demands.

Although my life in Czernowitz seems long ago, it has not been forgotten. Sometimes I wake up at night and I think that Father is dressing to catch the first tram. The memory of Father's departures in the darkness is still within me; whenever I think of them I feel sorry for him. Now we wake up together in daylight. The windows of the house are wide, and the light of snow streams inside. Two stoves blaze day and night, and I walk around the house without a sweater, unlike in Czernowitz. In the morning, we sit together at the table and drink coffee.

Every evening we go downtown, meeting Victor and my father's other old friends. Bucharest is bigger than Czernowitz, but colder. The sharp winter winds pounce on us from the alleys and lash at our faces. Of late, Father has changed beyond recognition. The depressions that he suffered from in Czernowitz don't appear to weigh on him here. Though he does drink and does speak enthusiastically, this is not the dangerous enthusiasm of Czernowitz. It's pleasant to be with him. When he's happy, everything around him seems happy—even the walls of the house. It's a pity he spends most of the day in the studio. When he emerges, he's as pale as chalk and immediately collapses in sleep. After two or three hours, he'll revive and we'll go out to the park. I don't dare to enter his studio when Father is at work. I think of his studio as an arena, where there are many demons in the guise of dwarfs. The demons are lithe and sticky, and they taunt Father. Father pulls them off, but they keep coming back, and they cling to him. I'd already heard about the demons in Czernowitz. Father would say— "Those demons!"—and make a gesture with his right hand. Even though I couldn't see them with my own eyes, I could feel their disturbing presence. Now it's clear to me: we've brought them from Czernowitz. In my heart of hearts, I pray that one day Father will muster the strength to push them far away.

We see Victor almost every evening. His stature and his clothes completely contradict his actions. From up close he looks like a poor, neglected man; his clothes smell of grease. He wears a striped blue suit that is faded and wrinkled; it's clear that he wears it all the time. It's strange—that the suit says more than his face: it speaks of his desperate attempts to help impoverished artists; it tells of nights without sleep. Father asks Victor if he painted in his youth. "Yes, I did paint," he replies, a smile stealing over his round face, "but heaven help those paintings!" Victor's impoverished appearance is misleading. On the day of our arrival he presented Father with a wad of banknotes, and every time he sees us, he gives more. Father says, "That's enough." But Victor cannot help himself. We sit in a café for two or three hours, sometimes till the last tram is about to depart, but we have not yet gone into a tavern. True, on our second day here Father equipped himself with some bottles. But here he drinks only at home.

Victor is planning a large exhibition of Father's paintings for the spring, to be held at the Raphael, a well-known gallery that is currently being renovated. "It's going to be quite an occasion," says Victor, his childlike eyes glowing. He has boundless faith in Father. I'm afraid of this faith, and I remember our last day in Czernowitz: Father tearing up sketches and paintings and shoving them into the gaping mouth of the stove. The landlord implores him, "Sir, don't destroy what you've made," but Father pays no attention to him and continues to rip up papers and canvases, feeding them to the fire with a fearsome glee.

One day Victor arrives at our house with a woman. She is tall and blond, and she has a smiling face. Father goes to greet them, and Victor introduces her as Suzy. Suzy is to come to us every day from nine to three to be Father's model.

"What is a model?" I ask Father at lunch.

"A woman whom one paints," Father replies, without raising his head from the plate.

Suzy appears the following day and enters the studio. I stand by the door and eavesdrop. "I'm twenty-nine and I've been married, but it didn't work out," Suzy tells Father. "Since I got divorced, I've modeled for two painters, and from now on I'll be happy to serve you, too."

Father asks some questions, and Suzy answers and laughs. Then they fall silent, and the only thing to be heard is the scratching of charcoal on the paper.

I go into the kitchen and sadness comes over me. It seems as though Father is also about to be taken from me, and I will be put into an orphanage. I decide that I will run away to Halina's village and await her resurrection there.

At three o'clock the door of the studio opens and Suzy comes out without looking at me. In the evening Father complains to Victor that it's hard for him to draw a woman who is also modeling for other artists. Victor asks why, and Father gives an example, and everyone at the café laughs. I understand nothing of what he has said, and yet I feel relieved.

This evening Father is in a good mood. He tells jokes and imitates people, and he narrates a long story about the famous art critic who at first had praised his work and then retracted what he'd said. Only a few days earlier Father had been mute, quite unable to produce a sound. Now he not only converses and expounds, but he even recites poetry and sings. In my heart, I pray that the demons that beset him in Czernowitz will not overcome him here. When the demons engulf him, his mood plummets, and depression darkens his brow and seals his mouth.

Suddenly Victor sinks to his knees and announces, "We will change the order of priorities."

"What priorities?" asks Father.

"Artists should be at the top of the ladder."

Father also sinks to his knees, and he embraces Victor; everyone laughs.

41

Victor has brought a new model to the house—a small and slender woman called Tina. Her expression is one of naïve wonder. Her lips tremble, and it's clear that speech doesn't come easily to her. I see at once that Father likes her.

I stare at Victor's round face. Sometimes he seems like a practical man whose actions are reflected in his every movement, and sometimes he seems so distracted that if truth be told, he doesn't know what he's doing. In the café, he eats sandwich after sandwich, and when it's almost midnight he says, "We have to go home; I've got a long day ahead of me tomorrow." It's not hard to guess that there's no woman waiting for him, and no hot dinner, and it's doubtful that he has changed his shirt in the past month. But he takes good care of us: every time he comes, he brings us vegetables and fruit, and a chocolate bar or box of candies for me.

Father works from morning till night. Through the door I hear the scratching of charcoal on the paper. Sometimes it sounds like he's trying to remove a stubborn stain from the paper. When Father paints I feel his efforts, and sweat covers my entire body. To share in his labors, I doodle on a pad and invent math problems.

Last night I dreamed of Mother. She was tall and full of

gaiety, and her hair spilled over her shoulders as it had during our summer vacation. But her eyes were listless. She spoke of the orphanage in which she had grown up. She had already told me something about it. Her parents died very young, and the Jewish orphanage had been her home. Now it could clearly be seen in her eyes that she was an orphan: they were sunk into their sockets, and the more I gazed into them, the more sunken they appeared. I woke up frightened; Father was in a deep sleep and did not hear me.

I remembered how run-down the orphanage in Storozynetz had looked, and pity filled my heart. Once I had asked Mother if she remembered her parents. "Nothing now," she said, and shrugged. Her words surprised me. Then I swore to myself that I would store in my memory all the people and the sights that have passed before my eyes, so when the day came I would be able to say: "Of course I remember. How could I forget?"

I get a letter from Mother today. Father doesn't ask me what she writes, but I tell him anyway. Mother wants to visit me at Christmas. Not a word about herself. I feel that even these few sentences did not come easily. I fold the letter and put it inside the writing pad.

Father is painting feverishly. The little woman appears each morning and emerges from the studio at three o'clock. Father's face has changed over the last few weeks, and in the evening, when he sits close to me, I feel the tension that simmers within him. I'm afraid of this tension and of his restrained movements. But even more than that, I'm afraid of the demons that surround him. The demons that were invisible in Czernowitz jump around here in every corner. Sometimes Father makes an abrupt gesture to drive them off, but they don't go far. I see them next to the sofa and beside the bed. They are very small beings in the shape of people. On the whole they are lively, but occasionally they fall prey to some kind of distress, and they shrivel up and disappear.

Yesterday Father let me come into the studio and showed me his paintings: demons—demons of every hue and kind. They were larger on the canvases than they were in our rooms. They had transparent human faces with expressions of mocking malice. The female demons are naked and rub up against the male demons provocatively.

"How are they?" asked Father.

I didn't know what to say. "Nice," I replied.

"It's not nice," said Father.

"What should I say?"

"You can also say nothing. You do recognize them?"

"I can see them clearly."

"Well, there you are!" he said, pleased that he had managed to explain something complicated to me. Suddenly I remembered that in Czernowitz Father had beaten up one of the critics who had called him "a prophet of doom who ought to be crucified."

That was the critic who brought the lawsuit against Father. The suit dragged through the courts for an entire year. Once, Father took me to the court, and I saw the lawyers for the defense and the prosecution wearing black gowns. Father was defended by a Jewish lawyer named Kurt Schnitzler. He would slap Father on the shoulder and say, "Don't worry, it will all work out."

Father gave the lawyer part of his salary every month, which completely drained his resources. Then, at the height of the litigation, the malevolent critic passed away. Father celebrated his demise with a drinking spree.

Father once told me, "As long as I breathe, I'll be beating up anti-Semites and art critics." But now he faces a different struggle. Sometimes it seems that he's painting the demons so as to expose their wickedness and their wretchedness, and sometimes it seems that he revels in their hidden wisdom. Father is a secretive person, revealing only part of his inner self, but there is a harsh honesty in everything he does.

In the meantime, winter is at its height, snow covers the fields, and we haven't left the house for more than a week. When Father comes out of his studio, his face and his clothes are covered with paint, and he reeks of turpentine.

42

In the midst of the winter storm Victor broke through the snowy siege and came to us. Two small horses harnessed to a narrow sleigh brought him, and with him, two baskets of provisions. "So long as there are people like Victor, it's worth living," said Father, in a burst of high spirits. Victor now looked a little more practical. His round face was ruddy and appeared firmer. Though he was as short as ever, he did not look awkward. He was happy that he had been able to reach us, and Father hastened to make him a cup of coffee. I've noticed that whenever he arrives, the demons scatter for dear life and the snow lights up the room.

Father showed him the paintings. Victor stood rapt, and as he looked at each in turn, he called out, "Splendid, splendid!" He told Father that the gallery was preparing to receive the pictures. The opening would be on the first of March.

Christmas arrived, and my hopes that Mother would visit me were dashed. She informed me by telegram: TO MY GREAT REGRET, I CANNOT COME. I was angry and vented my anger on the sketch pad; then I tore it up. Many of my father's habits were already in me. When I reach his age my face will be unshaven and my shirt creased, and there'll be a pen stuck into my coat pocket.

Mother changed in my mind's eye. Sometimes I saw her as a Ruthenian peasant woman, like those we saw washing or beating out linen by the streams of the Prut. Mother loved watching them work, as if she were searching for what she had lost. Sometimes I saw her as I did up close in Storozynetz, with the large briefcase in her right hand, hurrying to school. But mostly I saw her as she was during her last visit to me, in the heavy coat, walking slowly, her shoulders weighed down as if by a heavy insult. I so wanted to make her happy, but I didn't know how.

When Victor left the house, the demons surrounding Father returned. Sometimes it seemed that the demons were nothing but small animals that Father bred in cages and now found it hard to part with. "They must be driven out! They belong outside and not at home!" I wanted to blurt out, but of course I didn't. There were hours when they disappeared, when they were neither seen nor felt. Then it was clear to me that they existed solely in my imagination, and if I didn't imagine them, they wouldn't exist.

Whenever I asked Father about them, a smile would come to his face, as if I had asked him about his shifting moods. Once he said, "Demons? They're everywhere. Sometimes they dress up as moneylenders, and sometimes as art critics."

Occasionally he gave them nicknames: the red demon, the green one, the shriveled one. It was hard to know which of them were good and which wicked. Once I heard him say, "A demon is a demon."

It was strange how there, of all places, in that large and spacious house, they managed to annoy him more than in that sooty one-room apartment in Czernowitz. I tried to ignore them, telling myself, "They aren't real." But what was to be done? In spite of this, they seemed to appear wherever I turned. When I threw a wooden building block at them, or a spoon, they scattered in all directions. Sometimes they were so tiny that it was hard to see them, even with a steady eye. Once, Father stormed out from his studio, a rag in hand, threw open the front door, and shouted, "Get out! I don't want to see you anymore!"

One stormy, cold evening, Father explained to me that when an artist works, demons pounce on him, and he has to either ignore them or give them a good thrashing. When he spoke of them, he would emerge from his despondency and a smile would spread across his face, as if he accepted the fact that life is a continuum of unpleasantness, confusion, and malice, which nothing can change. But despite all this, life is still worth observing. Although observation changes nothing, it does divert the eye for a while.

Once, I peeked through the keyhole. The small woman was lying naked on the sofa. Father asked her something, and she answered in a mumble that sounded like a song. The sight was astonishing, and it was hard for me to tear myself away from the keyhole. I heard Father's voice. "My little demon, a bit to the right." The small woman leaned on the cushion with her arm, and her two large breasts spilled out from her body. Although I didn't see Father, I felt that he was gazing at her with great intensity. Another time I saw him drop to his knees and kiss her foot.

The furtive sounds in the studio reminded me of my walks with Halina, and how we sat by the water. Halina looked a little like the small woman. I had never seen her breasts, but I supposed that they were as beautiful as this woman's. Not that I could see Halina anymore, except in dreams, though whenever I saw a young woman in the street

I remembered her. Sometimes it seemed that soon I'd make the journey to be with her. Once, I reminded Father about Halina. Father shrugged, as if what I said was beside the point.

Suddenly Father emerged from his studio and called out in a despairing voice, "The exhibition opens on the first of March, and all I have is eight paintings." This new worry darkened his brow. Victor did not pressure him. He said in a quiet, friendly tone, "Whatever you have will be accepted gratefully." Father looked at him for a moment, as if not believing his own ears. Victor repeated, "There's nothing to worry about. What you've done is more than enough."

Father clenched his jaw and shut himself away in his studio. The snow fell unceasingly, and the small woman did not come. In the evening, when Father emerged from the studio, he looked like a growling lion. He muttered to himself, and he beat away demons to his left and his right. Once, in a white-hot fury, he said, "Art critics are ghastly demons — they should be exterminated." I did not understand what he was so angry about.

I'd already learned not to ask Father things when he's angry; there's terror in his fury. Here, too, I had seen him breaking planks. Sometimes I pictured him working in a circus, lifting heavy crates, bending iron bars, prizing chains apart, and riding on lions.

43

When Father is working, I wander from room to room, looking at all the photos on the walls. Though at first there seemed to be no particular order to them, I soon got to know that they're all about the life of the general. There's the general with his family, in elementary school, in high school, at the officers' academy. Then there are photos of the general in various elite units, being awarded medals for distinguished service, and, finally, the photo marking his retirement from the army. Victor's aunt isn't in these pictures; she made sure to hide herself. After the general became Jewish, he changed completely: he grew a beard and wore a skullcap. In one picture he is at a table poring over a book, and he looks just like one of the bearded Jews whom I saw in the synagogue in Storozynetz.

"Why did he become Jewish?" Father once asked Victor.

"It's a mystery to me."

"Did you ever speak with him about it?"

"I spoke to him, but I couldn't get it out of him."

I like the general. Sometimes I imagine him sitting in the synagogue in Storozynetz and praying and, without noticing it, imitating the gestures of the bearded Jews. Last evening I drew him and showed Father the drawing. Father laughed and said, "A Jewish general." There are expressions that amuse him, terms like "old Jew" or "half Jewish."

I try to draw Halina but the picture doesn't come. In Czernowitz I still saw Halina clearly. Since I've been here, her features have blurred. Father paints only what he can see, and because of that, all the demons and little imps have Tina's face. It's a shame that I didn't draw Halina when we were together. Had I done so, I could have kept her close to me. Now my memory plays tricks on me. Sometimes I feel like sitting and drawing what I see before me, so that when the time comes, my memory won't deceive me.

I want to ask Father many things, but he's just not there. He works away feverishly, and when he emerges from his studio he's so distracted that he'll ask strange questions; if the truth be told, he actually argues with himself. Victor begs him to put down his palette for an hour or two and go downtown, but Father won't hear of it. He swears that he will not stop until he's filled the quota he set for himself. Victor's face saddens for a moment, and he says, "What can I do?"

Last night we got a telegram from Mother: I'LL COME AT EASTER. Whenever I get news from Mother, my body trembles and my knees go weak. I've told myself so often: Mother is with André and I'm on my own, but I find it hard to stick to this separation. A telegram from Mother awakens my love for her, and I can't move. Not that Father is indifferent to a telegram from Mother. Although he doesn't look at what she's written, he'll ask, "What does Mother write?"

At Easter they crucified Jesus. After his crucifixion he rose again. Mother believes neither in God nor in life after death.

I've often heard her say, "Why do people say that God's in the sky? A person has to make his reckoning with himself, and not with God. Believing in God is foolish."

This kind of talk fills me with fear. It brings to mind pent-up anger and trying to burst through a locked door. When Mother left me with Halina, she warned her, "Don't tell him any tall stories about religion—they addle the brain." On hearing her injunction, Halina laughed. From the way she laughed, it was clear to me that she would not follow Mother's instructions, but would defy them at the first opportunity, as indeed she did. Halina loved telling me biblical stories about Abraham and Isaac and Jacob; the story of Joseph took days on end. I felt fear mingled with delight whenever she told me these stories; but I would sit beside her, listening.

Father's belief is a mystery to me. When I asked him if there's a God in heaven, he answered, "Supposedly."

For some reason, his answer saddened me.

44

In February the canvases smiled upon Father; he painted and was content. Tina's kindly face now peeked out from every picture. I felt sorry that she was surrounded by wicked demons and had to suffer from them, but apparently there's no happiness without pain. While Father was happy with his progress, adding paintings to his body of work, the owner of the gallery suddenly notified Victor that he would not rent out the hall to him, for he had been told that the artist painted decadent pictures. Victor explained—in vain—that it was great art, but the gallery owner not only remained unconvinced, he also threatened to notify the authorities.

I saw Victor and my heart sank. For some days he rushed around from one gallery to another. No one wanted to rent to him. In the end, he found a childhood friend who was prepared to put the downtown coffeehouse he owned at Victor's disposal.

Father went to see the place and was impressed. It was a coffeehouse of the old-fashioned kind, with high ceilings and wide windows. Father declared: "Better an honest coffeehouse than a splendid hall full of snakes." When Father makes declarations he's either drunk or close to being drunk; his arms lengthen and he waves them in wide circles.

The anti-Semites, at any rate, are everywhere, and Victor suffers from them as well. Even though his father had once been the deputy mayor and completely integrated in society, they don't let him forget that his mother had been Jewish and, what's more, a journalist with liberal notions.

We sat in a café and celebrated, and Father drank freely. But the episode had nevertheless left him with a bitter after-taste. Victor, eager to placate Father, brought us smoked fish, pickled cucumbers, and two loaves of country bread. Throughout the evening he kept speaking of the advantages of the coffeehouse and about the proprietor, who was one-quarter Jewish and who did his utmost to help.

Father continued to paint and his mood was even, but at night, when we went downtown, his face would darken and he'd rage: anti-Semites in every corner, all over the place, even in the pleasant coffeehouse where his pictures were going to be exhibited. Victor tried to calm him down, but Father refused to contain his fury, and whenever he ran into an anti-Semite he'd shout, "You filth! You bastard!" Sometimes Father seemed like a soldier fighting on two fronts. At home he fought against the demons, and outside, against the anti-Semites. Victor, it turned out, was more practical than Father. When Father was about to raise his voice, Victor whispered, "You have to ignore them." Clearly, Father could not do that.

At the end of February, Victor brought over a covered sleigh and he and Father piled the pictures onto it. Little Tina watched them. When the paintings had all been loaded and were covered in blankets, she suddenly burst into tears. Father rushed to embrace her and promised that from then on she would always be his model, and that the next week, right after the opening, he would start preparing a new exhibition. This promise stopped Tina's tears. Eventually she also climbed up onto the sleigh, and all of us went into town to hang the paintings.

It was not long after Father and Victor hung the paintings that the comments of the coffeehouse's clientele could be heard. Father restrained himself at first. But in the end he could no longer keep quiet and he began to shout.

The opening was the following evening. Victor's friends came, as did Father's admirers and a man named Karl Proper, whom I immediately saw was quite special. Father hugged him over and over again. It turned out that he was a famous art researcher. From Father's first exhibition he had been an admirer of his work. It had been a long time since I had seen Father as happy as he was that evening.

I sat next to Tina. Were it not for her large breasts, you would think she was a child. Now she looked down upon everyone from all the walls, at times in the form of a demon and at times in the form of a girl frightened of the demons.

"What grade are you in?" she asked me.

"I don't go to school," I replied. "I have asthma and Father got me exempted."

"And do you have a private teacher?"

"No, I learn from books and from workbooks."

Tina's face was filled with wonder, and she asked nothing more. I gazed at her for the entire evening, and the more I did so, the more enchanted I became.

I must have fallen asleep. After midnight Father carried me to the sleigh. In my sleep, I sensed his excitement and I heard him say, "My friend Victor pulled me up from the depths and restored my faith in God and in man. My thanks go to him both in this world and in the world to come."

He also mentioned Tina, saying, "She's right in front of

you. There is no flesh-and-blood artist who can compete with the Creator of the world. The Creator of the world should keep to himself and we'll keep to ourselves. And as for the gap—you can see it for yourself in my paintings."

Sometimes what you hear in sleep can be more lucid than what you hear when you're awake. But most of the time sleep is a barrier, and I pick up only the echoes.

45

The following day we went back to the coffeehouse to see if anyone had bought a painting. As it turned out, just one had been sold: Father's admirer, Karl Proper, had left his gold watch with the proprietor, promising to bring the money within a few days. The press summed up the exhibit in two words: Decadent Art. Father was furious and got drunk, shouting obscenities at the people sitting there. Victor and his friends barely managed to pull him outside. I clearly remember the complete havoc of this scene—it was the first time I had seen Father totally drunk. Victor never left his side, talking to him all the while. "Don't worry, I have enough money to put up seven such exhibitions. I'll buy the pictures and send them to France. In France, they still know real art when they see it." But Father did not calm down. Not even when he returned home did his rage abate.

Cold, gray days had come. Father stopped painting and slept for most of the day. I would go to his room almost hourly to look in on him. In the afternoon he would wake up and ask, "Where's Victor?" Victor would come in the afternoons and take us out to the country. Perhaps he thought that his being there would have a calming effect on Father, but of course in the country there's no good cognac, so we would come straight back to the city to stock up on a few bottles.

"I once loved the country," said Father distractedly.

"And now?"

"I find the quiet hard to take."

In moments of clarity, Father would embrace Victor and say, "What do you need this trouble for?"

There were some art critics, mostly Jews, who no longer wrote for the newspapers. They would come to see Father. But Father was not that welcoming, because he lumped all art critics together. Eventually people stopped visiting; only Victor came. Father would read the newspapers and say, "Here they are."

"They make no impression on me at all." Victor dismissed them lightly.

"Now they're telling us what to think."

"Telling who?"

Victor talked to Father softly, persuading and promising, stuffing banknotes into his pockets. One evening Victor came by with five of his friends and announced that the Pissarro Foundation's Committee for Visual Art had decided to award Father its annual prize. Victor hung a gold medallion around Father's neck as the five friends clapped. Father must have guessed that this was Victor's invention, but he was still happy. He drank, told jokes, and did not take the medallion off his neck the entire evening.

The next day Father did not get up to paint as I had expected, but slept until the afternoon. When he got up he asked, "Where's Victor?"

And Victor did come. Father asked if there'd been any interest in the exhibit. Victor told him that seven paintings had been sold so far and that there was considerable interest. Father looked dubious, but Victor put his hand on his heart. "I swear to God."

Then they sat in the living room, and Father suddenly asked about the general. Victor told him the story right from the beginning.

The general's wife, Victor's aunt, had been very unhappy when he converted to Judaism, but she was convinced that it was a passing whim. The poor woman could never have imagined that he would grow a beard and sidelocks, and that he would rise early every morning to go to the synagogue to pray. When she saw he was serious she threatened to leave the house, but eventually she gave in to his folly in the hope that one day he would revert to what he had been. His sudden death changed her, and she began to believe that his ancestors must have been Jews who were forcibly converted. She told not a soul of this conviction, except for Victor. Before her death she bequeathed all her property to him and asked Victor to turn the house, or at least one of its wings, into a museum, so that Jews could come and see how even famous generals can be drawn to the Jewish faith. The poor woman did not understand that the Jews themselves no longer wanted to live as Jews, and that nothing would help.

I loved listening to Victor speak about the general. A faint smile would play about his round cheeks. Father asked lots of questions, but Victor apologized bashfully, saying that he hadn't spoken with them all that much; his aunt had been a private woman and the general a stern man.

One morning little Tina came by and asked if Father was at home.

"He's sleeping," I whispered to her.

She immediately retreated to the doorway, apologizing. From sheer embarrassment I did not ask her to stay. The few encounters I'd had with her had instilled within me a closeness to her. Father, who was confused and angry at the time, had forgotten her, but I had not.

46

Winter grew more bitter with every passing day, and we hardly left the house. Victor would come by in the afternoons, bringing provisions and some bottles of cognac, and would tell Father how interest in his pictures was mounting and that it was time to start planning a new exhibition. It isn't easy to deceive Father. There are times when he's completely firm in his feelings and does not hide his opinions. "This isn't the time for art," he said.

"But there's the intelligentsia."

"I can't see it."

So now Father vented his anger—on the Jewish petite bourgeoisie, on anti-Semites, and on art critics of any ilk. To calm him, Victor took us out to a restaurant in the country. Here Father's rage subsided a little, and he talked about his childhood in the orphanage and his early exhibitions. The clouds passed over his face, and for a moment a youthful wonderment again shined in his eyes. His words flowed easily, and he didn't blame anyone. I saw Father as a young man borne from city to city on the shoulders of his admirers. The galleries in which his works are exhibited are full of people, and he's loved and admired by one and all.

Sometimes I thought that soon he'd go back to painting and that I saw signs of this. But I quickly learned that these signs were misleading. Father slept late and awakened angry—cursing, tearing up papers and tossing them into the fire. His face had changed over the past weeks: the anger had come to rest in his hands, and I was filled with fear that he'd strike someone again.

And, in fact, one evening when we were about to order dinner in a restaurant, the maître d' came up to us and asked us to move to a corner table. At first he claimed that the table had been reserved, but eventually he admitted that the other diners didn't want to sit near us, and he had to take their feelings into consideration.

"What defect do they find in us?" Father asked in a loud voice.

"I don't know."

"Let them move to a corner and not us."

"I insist that you move," said the maître d', in a tone that drove Father crazy. Father got up and, without further ado, hit him. The man rallied quickly and sprang at Father, who brought him down with a single punch. The restaurant's employees immediately gathered around and fell upon Father. Father took many blows and hit back, and he cursed in all the languages that he knew. Finally we found ourselves outside. Even now Victor did not lose his head. The incident amused him, and he threw himself into the snow, muttering and calling out, "Painters are strong, very strong; they know how to give as good as they get." Father did not laugh but went on cursing. In the end we went to the tram on foot. The walk calmed Father down, and he sang Ruthenian songs that he had heard in his childhood from the women who worked at the orphanage. And all that evening at home he sang these mournful Ruthenian songs, as if his soul had found a temporary refuge in them.

And so March passed. Father did not paint and did not read; he did not even listen to the news on the radio. Victor did not hide from us the fact that anti-Semitism was on the rise. One evening several walls were plastered with vicious slogans, and more and more the radio was full of venomous propaganda.

"We'll move to France," said Father.

"That's an idea," agreed Victor.

It was as if we were in a cage. Sometimes it seemed that Father was about to cause a huge scene that would topple houses and start a great conflagration. Victor would talk to him quietly, as if to someone who was sick and needed to be soothed. In the meantime, the demons had fled the house. I, at any rate, did not see them. But perhaps they had not been expelled, but were instead hiding in the cracks, and would emerge in the spring from their hiding places. Perhaps they were afraid of Father's rage and did not dare provoke him.

Last night Father surprised me and said, "We haven't heard a word from Mother. She promised to come and she hasn't."

"Mother promised to take me to the Carpathians," I reminded him.

"It won't work out this year. We're close to the end of winter. The snow is melting."

Later, Father told me that when he was young he had spent a month with a rich Jew who owned tracts of forests in the Carpathian Mountains. He had been hired to create paintings for the man's home, and he did begin to work, but when the rich man's wife saw the paintings, she clutched her head with both hands and shouted, "I don't want these paintings in my home—they depress me!" At first the husband tried to convince her that it was good art, showing her articles that praised Father's work, but it didn't help at all. So finally the rich man compensated Father with a substantial sum, and Father left. He told the story without bitterness, as if it were just a fleeting episode and not an unpleasant one.

47

While this was going on, I got a telegram from Mother: SICK WITH TYPHUS. CAN'T COME. LOVE YOU. MOTHER.

I showed it to Father. He read it and said nothing.

Victor came by in the afternoon, talking enthusiastically of the need to encourage real art as a shield against the darkness. Father didn't agree with him; he claimed that art no longer had a place in the face of the evil and vulgarity that had overtaken life. Victor's attempts to ease Father's despair were futile. "Bucharest is no different from Czernowitz," claimed Father, "and it's doubtful that the epidemic can be kept from spreading."

I was sad to see Father in such despair. Only a few weeks before, he had been happy and painting feverishly, but since the opening of his exhibition, he'd been angry, with furious words on the tip of his tongue. Now Victor took him only out to the country. They didn't bully us in country taverns, perhaps because they couldn't tell the difference between a Jew and someone from the city.

Then some of Victor's friends came to the house. They made toasts, joked around, and called the anti-Semites derogatory names. They spoke about the people running the country and about distant lands, and the heavy atmosphere lifted somewhat.

After the guests had gone, Father said, "We must set off immediately to see how Mother is doing."

"When?"

"As soon as possible."

It's hard to guess what Father's reactions will be. They're so sudden.

At first Victor tried to talk him out of the hasty journey, but when he saw that Father's mind was made up, he stopped. For a few days Father was caught up in a strange frenzy, tearing up papers and sketchbooks and talking about the need to arrange his life differently. "The house is yours," Victor kept promising. "Any time you'd like to return, just come."

Father didn't thank him but simply repeated, "Right now I have an urgent journey." The bottle of cognac was constantly on the table, and before uttering anything, Father would take a swig.

Just before we left, Victor came by and gave Father a wad of banknotes. He promised Father that he would buy any of the paintings that weren't sold in the exhibition and would send him the money anyplace Father wanted. Father was embarrassed. He shoved the banknotes into his coat pocket and thanked Victor with short bows. "As soon as Henia's health improves," he promised, "I'll rent a studio and I'll start to work."

We hardly packed for this trip. Father put my clothes into one suitcase and his into a duffel bag. The math books and the rest of the schoolbooks were left, for we both agreed that I wouldn't need them any longer. Victor was embarrassed, and he kept apologizing for the dismal atmosphere in the capital. Father was distracted. He kept patting his coat pockets and muttering, "I must first get to Storozynetz; when I'm there, I'll decide what to do."

Then Father sat in the living room with Victor, and I went from room to room. Since Father had decided on this journey, it had felt strange there, as though the spacious rooms filled with handsome things were about to be taken away from me and would soon be erased from my memory. I was sad about losing the visions of light that had been revealed to me there, and I tried to see them again so as to store them away inside me. But for some reason they resisted this, and my feelings were slowly being planted elsewhere.

Father got to his feet and said, "We have to go." Outside there was a fierce, snow-filled wind. Victor was sorry that he hadn't brought a sleigh.

"Don't worry," Father said, "it's not far to the tram, and we can do it in half an hour." His face was red, and he could hardly stand.

So we set out. On the way, Father told Victor about an art critic named Zeigfried Stein, who had written some nasty reviews of his early exhibitions. And as if this weren't enough, Stein then traveled to each place that Father's paintings were being shown, declaring publicly that this was dangerous, decadent art and should be banned.

"And what did you do?" asked Victor.

"I wanted to thrash him, but God got there first and shut him up."

"What happened to him?"

"He drowned in the river."

The train came on time. There were hundreds of people on the platform. Victor embraced Father, and tears coursed down his cheeks.

"Look after yourself." He spoke as if he wasn't Father's agent but his father.

"I promise you."

"You must paint," Victor persisted. "Every hour is precious."

"I'll get myself a studio first thing."

"Just telegram me and I'll send you anything you need."

"Thank you, my dear friend."

"Don't thank me."

"But I want to thank you."

"There's no need. Good-bye, dear friend. Don't forget to write me. I'm not going to budge from here."

And with these hurried words we parted from Victor and were pushed into our compartment. There were no longer any empty seats, and Father regretted not taking Victor's advice to buy seats in first class. He sat me down on the suitcase and stood next to me. I was tired, but I saw clearly the spacious house in which Victor had put us up, the chests of drawers, the wide beds, and the great light that streamed in from the large windows. Now it all seemed distant and imaginary, as if I hadn't ever been there.

I asked Father if we would return to Bucharest.

"Of course we'll come back. In Bucharest we have such a true friend. He'll welcome us with open arms whenever we come."

I sensed the trembling in his legs, and it hurt me that he had no place to sit down.

48

Then I fell asleep and I saw Mother. She was in a swimsuit, sitting alongside the stream and preparing a midmorning snack. Her face was clear and open, and a bright smile played upon her lips.

"Mother," I said.

She turned her head slowly toward me. I'd always known this way she had of turning her head, but now it was as if I were seeing it for the first time. I felt her love for me, and I was gripped by silence. She immediately explained that she'd wanted to come to me at Christmas and take me to the Carpathians, but things hadn't worked out. I didn't know what she was talking about, and I wasn't going to ask her. Her love was so apparent that it completely overwhelmed me.

"Mother," I said again.

"What, my love?"

"How long will we be here?" I tried to hold her attention.

"All the time," she replied after a brief pause.

"And I won't see Father anymore?" I asked, then regretted it.

"I, at any rate," she said in a tone that I recalled well, "intend to make the summer vacation last as long as I can."

"More than a year?"

"More than five years," she said, with a peal of laughter.

"And we won't leave here?"

"Why should we leave?"

"I thought perhaps we would travel to the city."

"What do we need the city for? The city destroys all hope."

"Hope." I tried to probe this familiar word, which suddenly sounded suspect to me.

"How else would you say it?" wondered Mother. This sentence was also something I recalled, but I didn't remember when it had been said.

Then I stopped talking and Mother prepared sandwiches. Her thin sandwiches, with yellow or white cheese. Mother's sandwiches had a fresh taste that they retained for hours.

"Why don't you ask me what I've been doing all this time?" I asked.

"I know everything."

"How?"

"I'm with you, even when you don't see me."

"So you know Victor?" I wanted to test her.

"Of course I know him. Victor was with me at the teachers' seminary. He was an outstanding pupil. But he didn't want to be a teacher; he was drawn to art."

"Strange."

"Why strange? He was always short and round and very generous."

After the meal we went down to the dark lake. The trees at the dark lake are always low and dense, protecting you on all sides, and we swam without clothes. Mother was taller without clothes, perhaps because she gathered up her hair. It was unusual for her to dive under the water and stay under so long. I was scared and shouted, "Mother!" Hearing my shout, she surfaced and floated.

When she came out of the water I started to ask her whether she had married André. Mother made a dismissive gesture with her hand, as if to say, "Let's not talk about it." But I couldn't hold back and I asked her anyway. Her face darkened and she said, "Why do you ask?" Her question, or, more accurately, her rebuke, was so sharp that it left me mute. She immediately added, "And suppose I did marry, is that a reason to lash me with knotted whips or banish me forever?"

I was shocked by what she said. "I love you, Mother."

"I hope so," she said suspiciously.

"Why do you say 'I hope so'?"

"What should I say?"

I didn't know how to respond, so I was silent.

"If I've been mistaken, do forgive me," said Mother in an affected tone of voice, which immediately saddened me.

We didn't speak the entire way home. Once inside, Mother took off her shoes and put them in the corner. Then she threw herself onto the bed and covered her face with her hands. I knew that I hadn't behaved well toward her, and yet my heart still did not let me go over to her. I stood in the doorway and watched her. The more I looked at her, the more I knew that she had been meaning to say something to me, but would not tell it to me now.

I woke up as the train came to a sudden halt, and I saw Father standing next to me. When he saw that I was awake, he knelt down and hugged me, as if he hadn't seen me for a long time.

49

Toward morning we reached Czernowitz, and we hurried straight to the café that Father loved, the Alaska. The proprietor gave us a warm welcome, calling out, "How come you disappeared on us, my dear fellow?"

"I've been in exile."

"Where in exile—if one might ask?"

"Everywhere outside Czernowitz is exile."

"If that's so, then you've been redeemed and you deserve a good breakfast."

And the breakfast came soon enough: toast, fried eggs, and cream cheese, to say nothing of the fragrant, hot coffee. The proprietor sat next to us, and Father told him about Bucharest, about the exhibit, and about the anti-Semites who had the city in their grip, casting terror in the streets and the cafés.

"Not that they're lacking here."

"But here they're quieter."

"That's what you think."

"In Bucharest they're swarming in every corner."

"And what did the art critics say?"

"Those critics are short and fat, and they are really asking for a good thrashing."

The owner burst out laughing and said, "Arthur is Arthur, and neither place nor time will change him."

After the meal, we went downtown to the Herrengasse. It was a bright, chilly day. Father was in good spirits. He unbuttoned his coat and walked about the cold streets as if it were spring. People were glad to see him and hugged him. I saw from close up how much Father loved his hometown, its people, and its language. Here, unlike in Bucharest, he was a native son; here everyone knew him by name and liked him.

At noon we entered the church refectory and ate corn pie with cream. Here, too, Father was greeted with gladness. People sang and cheered for Jesus, who promised redemption to all the faithful. Father gazed at those singing with great intensity, as if trying to engrave them onto his heart.

Then the venerable old man came in, supported by two young people, and silence fell upon the hall. He began by blessing those seated, praying that Jesus should dwell among them, that their eyes should see only good, and that they should judge all creatures favorably, for only on account of favorable judgment does the world exist. I liked the phrase "judging favorably," and I asked Father what it meant. Father put a finger to his lips, signaling silence.

The venerable man also talked about the poor, the downtrodden, and the sick, whom Jesus loves, saying that all those who help them support Him. Treat the poor well, for they shall bring redemption, the old man concluded, and then everyone stamped their feet.

After the meal I thought that we'd return to the railway station and travel to Mother in Storozynetz, but we didn't. Father met old friends and was glad to see them, and they convinced him to enter the tavern for a toast. Father yielded to temptation and went in.

At the tavern Father spoke at length about art and art critics, about the dealers' and gallery owners' monopoly, and about the dreadful taste of petite bourgeois Jews, who decorate their homes with sentimental works of art. He went on and on, and you could see that this was a place where he found a ready ear and where everyone respected him. Toward evening he got to his feet and said, "My dear friends, I must set out for Storozynetz."

"There's time; there's a night train." They sought to keep him there.

I was tired and fell asleep on the bench. When I awoke it was already night. Everyone was talking animatedly. Father stared at me suddenly and said, "My poor boy! Dragged around from pillar to post with his strange father and no corner to call his own. Let's take him straight to a hotel." He rose from his seat, pulled himself away from the gathering, and immediately set out with me for the hotel.

The owner of the hotel entered us in his registration book and told the bellhop to take our bags up to our room. It was a nice room, but it wasn't luxurious like our palace in Bucharest.

Father, it seemed, had drunk one glass too many. He spoke of things I didn't understand, and in the throes of his drunkenness, he swore that if an anti-Semite crossed his path, he would beat him without mercy. He also tossed out the name of some art critic whom he had mentioned before, but this time in a very direct and threatening way. Once I was afraid of Father's drunkenness, but now I wasn't. I knew that he'd eventually fall onto the bed, fold up his legs, and fall asleep.

Sometimes Father would wake up and call to me or one of his friends. I would hear but not answer—that's what he did at night and I wasn't frightened. Since we'd been together I'd come to know him well, from up close. Father was tall and strong, and sometimes I saw him in a dream, standing in a ring and boxing.

50

The following day we again did not rush to set out. Father was late getting up, and at noon we ate at the church refectory. After the meal we walked along the Prut. It was clear that Father loved the river and was happy to be near it. The entire way he hummed and spoke and argued, and eventually he turned to me and said, "Isn't it beautiful here?"

On our way back from the Prut, he met a friend from the orphanage. Father was glad to see him and immediately invited him to a café. A short, thin man, he was named Eddy. For years, since his youth, Eddy had worked at Frost's — a general store notorious for the ill treatment of its employees. He had tried other shops, but it hadn't worked out, and now he was thinking of emigrating to America.

"You're doing the right thing." Father spoke in a loud voice.

"For the time being, I'm saving for a ticket."

Father told him about Bucharest, about the exhibition, and about the anti-Semites swarming around everywhere.

"I can't imagine a world without anti-Semites." Eddy spoke in a clear but weak voice.

"I must have deluded myself all these years," said Father, imitating Eddy's voice.

"I don't even think about them."

"Why?"

"They're part of nature; apparently there's nothing to be done."

"And that's how it will always be?"

"That's how it seems to me," said Eddy, and shrugged like a child.

Father was stirred by his words, embraced him, and repeated over and over: "It's good I met you. How many years has it been since I've seen you? You haven't changed at all, Eddy."

"A pity that I can't change."

"Why do you say that?"

"A man has to change."

"You've already decided you're emigrating, and that's good."

"It's too late, my friend."

I noticed something: the skin on his fingers was transparent, and you could see his veins pulsing underneath. When he said, "It's too late, my friend," a look of wonder filled his large right eye.

Then Father asked about the store and its owner, and about Eddy's friends at work. Eddy replied at length, and Father, who is usually impatient, did not interrupt him. He questioned him in great detail, and Eddy answered in the same detail.

"And you?" Eddy suddenly raised his head.

"I'm going to Storozynetz. Henia—we no longer live together—has come down with typhus and is in the hospital."

Eddy lowered his head as if he was embarrassed that he had asked. Father added, "Henia worked at the primary school in Storozynetz. She's a dedicated teacher and was very highly thought of."

"May God make her well again," Eddy said in a voice that surprised Father.

"I see you're religious."

"Insofar as I can be."

"Strange," said Father, a smile cracking the corners of his mouth.

"Why strange?"

"We didn't have fathers to teach us."

"We did, only we didn't have the privilege of seeing them."

"I didn't know that you're religious," Father said again in a tone of wonder.

"I keep as much as I can," said Eddy without looking at us.

"As for me," Father confided to him, "I feel much closer to Christian rituals than to Jewish ones. Surely you remember how, at the orphanage, they would force us to pray. I couldn't stand the way we were forced."

"I also couldn't stand it," said Eddy in a quiet voice.

"And on Shabbos they didn't let us leave the yard."

"You remember, I see." Eddy laughed, and his large right eye filled his entire face.

Darkness began to fall. Father got to his feet and said, "We have to hurry to the train. It leaves at eight o'clock." Eddy, who had sat there hunched over the entire time, also got up. Now I saw clearly how thin and short he was, as if his orphanhood had not left him. Father took some banknotes from his wallet, held them out to Eddy, and said, "That's from me toward your ticket to America."

"What's with you?" said Eddy, stepping back.

"It's nothing."

"I won't take it."

"I beg you to."

"I can't."

"You must take it," said Father in a tone that shocked me.

"And if I don't travel to America?" said Eddy in a different tone of voice.

"Then you'll give it back to me."

Father had apparently put him on the spot, and Eddy seemed frozen in place. He stood there in silence, his head bent, and then he began to cry. At first it looked like he was shedding only a few tears, but the longer he stood there, the more the weeping spread throughout his body, making his shoulders shake.

"Forgive me," said Father, and slipped the banknotes back into his coat pocket.

"*You* have to forgive *me;* I've refused your generosity."

And so they parted. Father and I headed down to the station, and Eddy turned and went on his way. Father tried to explain it all to me, but I didn't understand anything he said. I felt that Eddy's refusal to accept his money had hurt him. As always after a hurt, Father raised his collar and buried his head inside it.

51

We missed the eight o'clock train and waited at the snack counter for the one departing at midnight. Father read a newspaper, lighting one cigarette from another. A cold night already crouched over the empty platforms. Here and there a porter could be seen dragging a bag or a suitcase. The warehouses alongside the platforms were locked with wide iron bars, and dim light rested on the protruding window-sills. I suddenly felt so sorry for Father that I touched his hand.

"What is it, dear?" He turned to me apprehensively.

"Nothing, Father."

I saw how his speech had become muted and his cheeks sunken. People came and went, but there were no familiar faces among them.

After an hour and a half's delay, the train arrived. The car was cold and empty. The suitcase and the duffel bag seemed small next to the seats, as if they had shrunk. Father wrapped me in a sweater and took off my shoes. The lights from the lamps came through the windowpanes, laying squares of light on the floor.

"Are you cold?" Father asked in a whisper.

"No."

"In three and a half hours we'll be in Storozynetz."

The words echoed through the empty car and then vanished. Father took a few swigs from his flask, and a groan escaped him. I again saw Eddy, from whom we had parted only a short while earlier. His large right eye was spread over his face, as if it was trying to hide his soul. Now I understood: Eddy had not cried over Father's fate but over himself and his own life, which had not changed since he had left the orphanage.

I was awake. The wide car was full of shimmering shadows that heightened my alertness and overwhelmed me.

Later I fell asleep, and I saw Mother emerging from brackish water. It was similar to what I had seen in the summer—the river flowed in the same direction, and the water was black and viscous.

"Mother!" I called.

"What is it, my dear?" she said, and the black water flowed away from her. Some water stains clung to the upper part of her body.

"Mother, please take away those stains."

"It's nothing," Mother said, and shook them off, the way she shook dust off her coat. Now it seemed that she was about to kneel down, spread out a cloth, and prepare sandwiches. These movements are imprinted in my mind, and I can easily imitate them.

But this time she did not spread out a cloth; instead she drew out of her bag the books and notebooks that I had left in Victor's splendid home in Bucharest, laying them on the ground. For some reason they seemed very tattered, as if someone other than I had been studying from them.

"Mother, did you bring all this here?" My mouth dropped open.

"It wasn't heavy," she said, and showed me the bag.

"And you didn't bring sandwiches?" I asked, and immediately regretted my question.

"I did prepare them," she said, "but they spoiled."

"They got black?" I asked.

"How do you know?"

I looked at the water. It flowed black, and in the bends of the river, a sharp metallic light glinted on its surface. Mother wasn't surprised by all this oddness; on the contrary, there was a strange ease about her.

"Mother." I raised my eyes to her.

"What is it, my dear?" she said.

"I know that you've married André," I told her.

"How do you know?"

"Everyone knows."

"But you weren't supposed to know."

"If everyone knows it, so do I," I said, and we both laughed, as if we had been caught in a white lie.

52

We reached the station at Storozynetz early in the morning. Frost sparkled on the ground and on the platforms, and icicles hung on the drainpipes, but the sky was blue and clear, and a large sun appeared on the horizon.

"I need a cup of coffee; that's just what I need," said Father, stomping his feet.

Here, too, there weren't many people. What few there were hurried to the front entrance. Someone shouted, "Where are you?" But there was no response.

Seeing the station and its familiar entrance cheered me up. For a moment it seemed that we had come here only to drink our morning coffee at Café Vienna, renowned for its splendid cakes, and then go off somewhere else. The café owner, who did not remember us, turned to us and said, "Gentlemen, you're up early today. The first rolls won't be coming out of the oven for another half an hour; why not read the paper in the meantime."

Alongside the partition between the café and the bakery was a counter beyond which you could see the fiery oven. In the hall itself, the dimness of night still reigned. The proprietor returned, promising that coffee and cake would soon be served.

Father lit a cigarette. I clearly remembered coming here with Mother. She was wearing a blue poplin dress. We sat next to the window, and it felt like a continuation of our summer vacation. I had no idea at the time that it was only a prelude to those long and meandering days, that I would lose Halina, and that Mother would find herself a lover. Disaster seemed distant then, as if it belonged to other people and not to me.

The cheesecake arrived and with it steaming coffee. Father tasted it and said, "Excellent." The grayness in his face faded away, and only traces of it remained under his eyes. The café owner came over and offered us another cup of coffee. Father said, "Of course." He praised the coffee and the cake.

"I used to come here with Halina." The words popped out of my mouth.

"Who?"

"Halina."

"I don't remember her."

"Halina. The girl who was killed."

The word "killed," which had never before passed my lips, was like a flare in my memory. I immediately saw the funeral, with flutists playing all the way from the village to the graveyard. I also saw the clear skies opening to receive Halina. Because Mother had been in a hurry to get back, we didn't attend the funeral meal and didn't see her full resurrection. I was angry with Mother: she was head over heels in love.

Father asked the proprietor how to get to the hospital; he stood in the doorway and pointed, saying, "Straight ahead, straight ahead."

It was hard to grasp that we were about to visit Mother, sick in the very same place where Halina had been. I saw only Halina, as if both the place and the way to it belonged to her. Father didn't speak, and I didn't disturb him. Winter still crouched everywhere, and we walked along slowly, as if we weren't in a hurry.

In the hospital forecourt many homeless people lay around and thin dogs strayed among the low carts. The homeless were momentarily taken aback when we appeared, and shouted, "Jews!" Father stood there and stared at them.

"Jew, what are you looking at?" one of them said.

Father strode over to him, and the man fled for dear life.

We entered the corridor and climbed the steps. The man at the desk apparently remembered me, but responded with a shrug to Father's question. "Not with us. Perhaps at Wexler's, the private hospital. Or perhaps at the monks' hospice."

"Where is the Wexler hospital?"

"Not far."

As we left, one of the homeless shouted out rudely, "What are you doing here, Jew?"

Father didn't hesitate. He grabbed the man by his coat and shook him. The man must have been shocked by Father's reaction and said, "I didn't mean you."

"So who, then?"

"The bearded Jews."

"Ask forgiveness. Apologize right now."

"I'm asking."

"That's not how you ask."

"What should I say?"

"Say: 'I ask forgiveness of all Jews.'"

The man repeated this word for word, and Father let him go.

"Run for it!" his friends urged him, but the man stood where he was, as if in the grasp of paralysis.

53

We set out in search of Dr. Wexler's hospital. Suddenly I saw Mother as she was back in Czernowitz. She was wearing a thick coat and her steps were heavy and cumbersome; she looked like an old peasant woman. I wanted to rub this image out of my eyes, but it was stuck there.

We asked passersby about the hospital. No one knew Dr. Wexler, and those who had heard of the hospital did not know how to direct us there. Finally we found a Jew who showed us the way and blessed us. The sun rose into the horizon, lighting up fields and trees that were bare of leaves. The white snow had disappeared, but clumps of gray snow still lay along the fields. In the distance small peasant cottages could be glimpsed, thin trails of smoke rising from their chimneys.

We reached Dr. Wexler's hospital by midday. It was a two-story structure, with a guard at the entrance. To Father's inquiry as to whether a woman by the name of Henia was a patient there, the guard scanned a list and responded with a decisive "No." We didn't know Mother's new surname, and so Father asked to see Dr. Wexler. The guard stood up and said, "Dr. Wexler is busy examining patients at the moment and cannot see anyone."

"When will he be available, sir?"

"I don't know."

Father put down the suitcase and the duffel bag and lit a cigarette. I saw the anger coursing through his hands, and I was afraid. I used to think that when Father got angry he broke only furniture. Now I knew that he was liable to raise his hand and start hitting people.

Father asked the guard if it was a long way to the monastery hospital.

"It's far."

"And can one rent a wagon?"

"No." The guard answered briefly and reluctantly; it must have enraged Father. Father went up to him and warned him with a look, but apparently the man had no idea what Father was capable of and said, "Get out of here!" Father hesitated no longer and smacked him. Then he went straight in, dragging me with him and leaving the bags outside.

The staff must have seen what Father had done, and they stood there, cowed.

"I'm looking for a patient called Henia," said Father wildly.

"We don't have a woman by that name," replied a woman in a choked voice.

"How many patients do you have?" Father continued in the same wild vein.

"Twenty-four."

"I want to see them."

A door opened and there stood Dr. Wexler. A tall, thin man, he sized us up with a cool, restrained gaze. In response to his question about what we wanted, Father's answer rang out clear, "I'm looking for a patient by the name of Henia, and I want to know if she's here."

"Her surname?"

"We don't know."

Dr. Wexler must have seen that Father would not be swayed because he said, "There is nothing to hide; we'll show him everything." We went from ward to ward and saw all the patients, with their sickly, frozen expressions. Mother was not among them.

"These are our patients," said Dr. Wexler, and stepped back.

"Has no one been released in the past few days?"

"No one."

"I'm sorry," said Father, and grabbed my hand.

"Thank God that there *are* things that can be ascertained," said Dr. Wexler.

Father made no comment, and we went out.

On the way, Father talked and talked, trying to prove to me that everything was the guard's fault: he had been rude and had shouted; he had wanted to throw us out. Had he but spoken politely, Father would not have had to hit him, and everything would have gone fine. "Those guards really like to lord it over everyone; they need to be taught a lesson."

Still, he wasn't pleased with what had happened, for after he had explained himself to me, he fell silent and buried his head in his coat. He didn't utter a word all the way back to Storozynetz.

We went into a restaurant. Father ordered borscht with cream and corn pie and asked the woman who owned the place how far it was to the monks' infirmary.

"It's not that far, but the road is terrible and very winding; you'd be better off renting a wagon."

"There's a wagon here for rent?"

"Of course there is," she said, and revealed a mouth full of small teeth.

"Would you be so good as to order us a wagon?" Father said to her, as if trying to placate her.

"I'll do it gladly," she replied, and left to prepare the meal.

The dishes were tasty, and Father asked for more.

"Strange," said Father.

"What's strange?" I asked.

Father lifted his head from the plate and did not answer my question. His forehead was clear, as was the area around his eyes, but it still seemed to me that he was tormented by thoughts that gave him no rest.

For dessert, the owner brought us plum compote and said, "This is on the house." Looking at her, I saw that she liked her guests and wanted to make them happy. There was a purity in her expression. Father asked if she had ordered the wagon.

"I certainly did, and it's waiting for you." She spoke in a child's voice.

"Thank you," said Father.

"It's nothing," said the woman, in a voice that reminded me, for some reason, of another woman.

54

We set out toward evening. The restaurant owner was right: it really was a winding, precipitous road, and we dismounted from the wagon several times to make it easier on the horses. The driver cursed both the steep ascent and the horses. Father held out the flask to him, and he took more and more swigs. In the end he turned toward us and asked, "You're Jews, aren't you?"

"Correct," said Father with emphasis.

"What's with Jews at a monastery?"

"We have someone sick at the infirmary."

"A sick Jew?"

"You'd suppose," said Father in an affected tone.

"And still, what's with Jews at a monastery?"

"Jews also believe in God," Father replied in a different tone of voice.

"Not the new Jews."

"The new ones are not that different from the old ones."

"Completely different," the peasant said firmly.

"In what way?"

"The new ones don't pray."

"And what else?"

"They don't fast on Yom Kippur."

"What's wrong with that?"

"People who have no God are frightening."

"Who do they frighten?"

"Us."

"They don't frighten me." Father made a funny gesture.

"True," said the wagon driver.

"Why 'true'?"

"Because sir's apparently one of them."

Father laughed. The driver's wit had caught him off guard, and he said, "I see you know Jews well."

"I grew up with them."

"With the old Jews or with the new ones?"

"Both of them."

"Which do you prefer?"

"The old ones keep to themselves, and the new ones travel to the city to learn medicine."

"True, true." Father laughed again, and it was clear that the wagon driver's insights amused him.

We reached the monastery with the last light. Father asked about the cost of the journey, and the driver named his price. Father doubled it and handed him the banknotes. The wagon driver was astonished. He shook his head and smiled.

We got down from the wagon and stood at the gate.

"May God bless you," the driver called out from his seat.

"And you, too," Father replied in the same tone of voice.

I immediately saw that this was a different place from the ones I had seen till now. A tall monk stood at the entrance to welcome us, and Father hastened to explain why we had come. The monk listened, and I saw that his attentiveness not like ours. "You're looking for Henia Drushenko?" The monk wanted to be sure.

"Correct."

"She is, indeed, in our infirmary."

"And may we see her?"

"I should think so."

I looked up and saw that the entrance was decorated with pictures of saints and that the windows were of stained glass. From the nearby hall came a burst of organ music accompanied by a choir of male voices.

"I'll take you to the waiting room," said the monk, and we went straight down a long corridor that was lit with tall wax candles. At its end there was a spacious waiting room. "Please be seated. You'll be called," said the monk, and he retraced his steps.

Here the music could not be heard. From the long, narrow, stained-glass windows, a blue light streamed into the hall. The silence was so thick you could almost touch it.

"How do you feel?" asked Father, taking my hand.

"I'm all right," I said. I was not afraid, but I had the feeling that this hall led to a long corridor, just like the one we had passed through, and at the end of it there was another hall, just like the hall we were sitting in. For some reason, this thought made me dizzy, and I closed my eyes.

Father got to his feet and went to look at the paintings on the walls. He liked them, and he smiled faintly, the way he always did when he was satisfied with some picture or object.

I closed my eyes and saw the road that we had taken with the wagon driver. The driver's behavior had not been pleasant. He had cursed and lashed at the horses without mercy, but Father had not been angry with him. The responses the driver gave Father had amused him, and he had smiled and laughed the entire way. Even now, as he stood next to the pictures, a trace of that same smile played on his lips.

"They've forgotten about us." Father turned to me. "Good that there are ancient pictures here that one can look at. These old pictures are always amazing, because they don't try to be more than what they are—do you understand?" I did not understand, but I didn't dare ask him to explain. Most of what Father says is beyond me, and yet still I like to hear it.

55

A little later, a monk entered and Father introduced himself. "Arthur Rosenfeld. I used to be married to Henia. And this is her son."

"Henia is very sick." The monk did not hide the truth.

"Is she talking?" Father asked.

"Very seldom, only when she opens her eyes."

"We would like to see her." Father spoke in a quiet voice.

"Come with me."

Again we went down a long corridor that was lit with tall wax candles. Here and there in the arched ceiling there'd be a dark skylight. For some reason, I suddenly recalled Tina's small, wondering face, when Victor and Father had loaded the suitcase and duffel bag on the sleigh. Her wonder had been intense, as if she realized that from now on her life would no longer be what it had been. I tried to uproot this memory from my mind and think only about Mother. But my efforts were futile; only when Father held out his hand to me did I understand that at the end of the corridor we would stop, drop to our knees, and fall to the floor.

The monk stopped walking, and we found ourselves standing next to a white iron bedstead. In the bed lay a woman, her head sunk into a pillow and her eyes closed. I did not recognize her, and neither did Father. "That's Henia?" he asked falteringly.

"Yes, sir."

"Henia," whispered Father. The woman in the bed did not move. Father turned his head, as if looking to see if anyone was behind him, and approached the bed.

"Does Henia open her eyes?" Father asked in a subdued voice.

"Sometimes."

"We have come from far off, from Bucharest. The bad news caught up with us there, and we immediately decided to come here. There are things that a person must do." Father spoke distractedly.

"I understand," said the monk.

I had the feeling that Father was not speaking to the point, and that the monk would soon interrupt him to point out his mistake. The monk did in fact change the tone of his speech; he turned to Father and asked, "Where will you spend the night?"

"We would like to return to Storozynetz."

"It's late, good sir, and it's doubtful that a wagon can be found."

"And is there an inn in these parts?"

"There is, sir."

"Very good," said Father, as though he had finally found the solution to a mystery.

And so the visit was more or less over. The monk turned and we followed him out. At the entrance he showed us the way to the inn.

"Sir." Father turned suddenly to the monk and said in a practical voice, "What has Henia got?"

"Typhus, sir."

"And since then she hasn't opened her eyes?"

"She's opened them, sir."

"And what did she say?"

"She muttered disjointed words, which none of us could understand."

Father lowered his head, as if the monk was not talking but lashing his head with a whip.

The walk to the inn took about half an hour. Father said nothing; he mumbled to himself and finally asked me if I was cold. I knew that as soon as he got to the inn he would order a drink, and that's what he did. After he had gulped it down, he rubbed his hands, turned to me, and asked, "What shall I order for you, dear?"

I asked for a fried egg with bread and butter. I was tired, and what I had seen that day returned to me. The thought that Mother was very sick and lying in a monastery did not preoccupy me. It seemed that our staying here was a preparation for another journey, a longer one, to a place where we would meet Mother again. Father downed some drinks and his mood picked up. He asked the innkeeper about the monastery and the infirmary. The innkeeper did not hold back his opinion. "Corrupt to its very foundations."

"The monks or the workers?"

"Both the monks and the workers."

"Strange," said Father. "You'd expect that a holy place would be pure."

"There is no purity in this world, you mark my words," said the innkeeper, exposing a mouthful of white teeth. After that Father sat with him, and they chatted like old friends. But then, suddenly, one of the drunks got up, came over to our table, and called out, "What are Jews doing in this holy place?"

"Jews are people, too, and God dwells also in their hearts." Father spoke as peasants speak.

"Who said that the Jews are also people?"

"I said it," said Father.

"I say that they are devils."

"I'm not a devil," said Father. "I'm flesh and blood, and I'm just like anyone else."

"Ah—there's the lie."

"What lie?"

"There's the lie." It was clear that the peasant had no more words, and that he would only repeat the same ones with different emphasis. The innkeeper, who just a few moments before had talked with Father in such a friendly way, did not intervene. He must not have caught on that Father was Jewish; when he realized it, he held himself aloof.

In the meantime, more drunks gathered around our table. There were no blows, only empty threats. Father shouted, "All anti-Semites will have to give account, and the day will come when they'll be put into the same prison in which the art critics are put." Everyone laughed and laughed, waving hands and bottles. The tumult went on for a long time. Finally the drunks dispersed, and Father turned to ask the innkeeper if there was a room for the night.

"There is," said the innkeeper unenthusiastically.

"We're dead tired," said Father. I was completely exhausted, and yet I still caught the phrase "dead tired," and I repeated it to myself until it penetrated the darkness of my head.

56

The following day we returned to the monastery. The monk at the entrance and the monk in the waiting room both welcomed us and bowed, and soon we were standing by the white iron bed. Now I recognized Mother's face. Her hair had grayed and her cheeks were sunken, but her smile, or what remained of it, hovered about her lips.

The monk left, and the two of us stood there. A pure light streamed in from the windows and washed over the pictures and the statues that were set into the walls. I knew Mother's sleep, but this wasn't her sleep. Her head was sunk deep into the pillow, and a strange paleness covered her face.

The longer we stood there, the clearer it became that we would not be able to draw Mother out of this deep sleep. Father took a firm hold of my hand and said, "Let's go." But the moment he uttered those words, Mother opened her eyes and looked at us. "Arthur," she said, and immediately closed her eyes again.

We remained by the bed, Father on his knees and me at his side. We heard the praying of the monks and the choir accompanying them. I saw angels hovering in the sky and felt that I, too, was ascending.

The monk came back to us, and Father told him that

Mother had opened her eyes, recognized him, and spoken his name. "That's a good sign," the monk said, and we left with him.

"And where is her husband?" asked Father in a chillingly practical voice.

"They've parted."

"I didn't know."

"The headmaster from her school came once."

"And no one else?"

"No one."

We went outside, walked around the monastery, and then returned to the inn. It was empty, and we sat next to the window. Father had a drink and I ate a sandwich. The long journey now seemed like a dream taking place in a steep valley with no way out. Father's attempts to get out proved futile; the walls were sheer and the canyon narrow as we went forward.

Father could not calm down. We returned to the monastery, and the monk at the entrance told us that Mother had been brought there a month ago, critically ill. The doctors had taken care of her, but although her situation had improved, her life was still in danger.

"What can we do?" Father asked with an exaggerated gesture.

"Pray."

"And if we don't know how to pray?" asked Father, using the plural for some reason.

"Don't worry, sir, we'll do that on your behalf."

"I thank you with all my heart," said Father, as if the man had removed a heavy weight from his shoulders. But it seemed to be only a temporary relief. Father was angry, and mostly with himself. The journey to Bucharest and the exhibition now seemed to him like a nightmare.

We circled the walls of the monastery again. The walk was long and tiring, and toward evening we returned to the inn. Now it was full. The smell of vodka and tobacco hung densely in the stale air. Suddenly, a man emerged out of the tobacco smoke and approached Father. Father did not recognize him at first, but then he fell on his neck and cried out, "Kuba!"

Kuba had been Father's friend at the orphanage, and they had studied painting together at the academy. His first exhibit was held at the Raphael Gallery, and he had made a name for himself. A year later, he disappeared. Rumor had it that he had sailed to America. Now the mystery was solved: Kuba had bought a house in the Carpathians and retreated there to lead a life of piety. Kuba now looked like one of the Jews whom I had seen in the synagogue at Storozynetz; his beard was long and thick, and he wore a peaked cap. He came into town once a month to stock up on provisions. Father asked if he had a family, and Kuba replied immediately: six sons and a daughter.

We went out to his wagon, and Father helped him load up the provisions. Then he told Kuba about Mother and her illness, and about the long sleep into which she had sunk. Kuba's body seemed to shrink with the bad news, and he closed his eyes. Father said, "I will be here until the doctors draw her out of her deep sleep."

They stood there, talking, recalling people and places and, of course, the orphanage. Kuba seemed to listen with his entire being, and he kept embracing Father and promising to come and see us. For a long time we stood watching his wagon as it disappeared in the distance. And we were silent, as if something wondrous had befallen us.

57

We went back to see Mother the next day, and we were astonished. Mother was sitting up, leaning against two heavy pillows, her eyes wide open. Father sank down onto his knees, and I followed him. Mother's face was turned toward us, but her gaze was somewhere else. "Henia," whispered Father, but Mother did not respond. The elderly monk who was standing next to us and who was a witness to the miracle also sank to his knees. Father pressed both his hands to the floor, as if he were trying to push himself up.

Suddenly, Mother shut her eyes and her face closed. The monk looked at us as if to hint: it's best to leave her; the patient needs complete rest. Father got to his feet, and I did as he did.

"She's feeling better," said Father.

"True," said the monk.

"Thank God," said Father, as if he had borrowed these two words from the monk.

We stood there, looking at her. Her closed eyes seemed to be gazing inside herself.

The monk turned toward the door, and we followed

him out. Almost without realizing it, we walked down the long corridor and found ourselves outside.

"She must be better?" Father linked his question to the monk's answer.

Again we circled the monastery. Before we had completed the walk, Father said, "Mother will get better and we'll take her with us to Czernowitz. Her marriage to André was a mistake." His voice was devoid of anger and rang clear. As if I was in a sweet twilight, I now remembered the apartment that we had lived in together with Mother, with Father sitting on the floor and playing dominos with me.

How many lifetimes had we been through since then? My bond with Father had deepened in the past year. His silence no longer weighed upon me. I could walk with him for two or three hours without exchanging a word and at the end of the walk feel that we'd talked a lot.

We ate lunch at the home of a peasant, who served us corn pie and omelets made with cream that he had just skimmed off sour milk. We were hungry, and we ate with relish. Father paid, and the peasant asked if we were Jews.

"You've got it wrong," Father rebuked him. "We're Swabian; you can't see that we're Swabian?"

"My mistake," he apologized.

"You don't see that we're taller than Jews?" Father did not let up.

"You can see it."

"So how did you make such a mistake?"

"It just seemed to me—"

"Not every person who speaks German is a Jew."

"You're right, sir."

I liked Father's charade. When he was in a good mood he entertained, told jokes, and threw in the occasional vulgar word. There were times when he would put on a peasant's hat or a merchant's hat, doing imitations and playing entire scenes, and everyone would hang on to every word that came out of his mouth.

So it was then. Father sang, climbed a tree, and imitated the peasant at whose home we had eaten and the innkeeper at whose inn we were spending the night. Most of the time I was afraid of his happiness. After such happiness, darkness would descend upon him, his eyes would narrow, his head would retreat into the collar of his coat, and not a sound would come out of his mouth. But on that day his high spirits did not plummet. He took gulps from his flask, and until late into the night he told me about his childhood in the orphanage and about how he had met Mother.

That night I dreamed that we were traveling on the train, passing stations in the semidarkness. A man who sat next to Father was pestering him with questions. At first Father was polite and answered, but when the man overdid it, Father got to his feet and shouted, "Enough! I don't owe you any answers!" The man was taken aback by Father's tone of voice but continued asking his questions. Father ignored him, but the man did not let up. Father warned him that if he continued to bother him he would hit him, but the man ignored his warning and laughed. That laughter seemed to hurt Father deeply, and he struck the man in the face. Then the man got up and called out, "I've exposed the face of this Jew!"

Father continued to hit the man. His punches, though strong enough, apparently did not hurt him, for the man continued to laugh, as if he wasn't the one being beaten but the one doing the hitting. And indeed he was. I lifted up my eyes: Father's face was covered with blood.

58

Our life now revolves around the monastery. We come to see Mother at regular times. Sometimes Father falls to his knees and does not stir from that spot for an entire hour. Sometimes Mother opens her eyes and gazes at us, and sometimes a word escapes her. But for the most part she's sunk in her sleep, and we stand by her bed and gaze at her. It's Mother and yet not her. She looks at us but does not see us. Sometimes I feel that she tries to pull us into her sleep. I would go to her willingly, but I do not know how to break through the barrier between wakefulness and sleep. Father seems to know a little about it. I heard him discuss this with one of the monks. An elderly monk heard Father's name and cried out in wonder, "Why, if it isn't Arthur Rosenfeld—the famous painter?!" It turned out that this elderly monk loved painting; he had seen Father's exhibitions, admired them, and bought a small sketch that he hung in his room. He even remembered that one of the critics had called Father the King of the Demons—even then Father frequently painted demons. But Father doesn't usually talk with the monks about painting; they talk, instead, about the mystery of faith. It's hard for me to understand these complicated things, and I stand in awe as Father converses with the monks as an equal. Sometimes he recites poems or passages from the Bible to the admiring monks. Once I heard one of the monks say to him, "You're really one of us. How did you come to live in a world without God?" Father answered him straightforwardly, "There's no man without God," much to my surprise.

On clear days we venture farther, to the forest or the open fields. Our walks are mainly journeys of silence, but once, Father turned to me and said, "Don't take the path I've taken." I asked him what he meant. He answered me at length, but I understood nothing of his explanations.

The days pass, and there is a strange order to our life here. Sometimes it seems that this is how it will be from now on, forever. Occasionally, after a visit to the monastery, Father may burst into tears, his whole body trembling. I don't know what to do and I stand next to him like a block of wood.

In the midst of this, Kuba, Father's friend from the orphanage, arrives. He has brought us dried fruit and pear preserves made by his wife. He very much wants us to come visit him in the hills, but Father holds firm. "I cannot leave this place. My duty is to be here right now." Kuba is a head shorter than Father, his face dark and his eyes sunk in their sockets. When Father talks, Kuba's eyes open very wide and he absorbs the words with them. Father loves that he is here with us, and he constantly gazes at him.

We go into the inn, and Father tells Kuba that here the monks have retained the ancient traditions; they don't eat pork and they bury their dead on the day of their death. Kuba listens but doesn't ask for details. Father goes on drinking and appears to become drunk, for he talks at the top of his voice. Among many things, he tells Kuba about the wonderful people God had put in his path, like the

Ruthenian peasant with whom we lodged, who loved Jews more than life itself and who for months refused to take any rent from him because he was a Jew, for Jews are the sons of kings and they're hidden priests and they need to be helped to carry out their hidden purpose in the world. Then he tells Kuba about the amazing Victor, who put a mansion at his disposal and arranged an exhibition for him, ignoring the anti-Semites. He mentions how much Victor loves his fellow men and loves artists, how he fought for their cause with all his might and put his entire wealth at their disposal. "God has put many good angels in my path. He even put Henia in my path, but I didn't know how to look after her and now she's lost to me."

So Father talks, and the more he talks, the simpler the sentences become, and even I understand them. Kuba listens, large tears flowing from his wide-open eyes, but he utters not a word.

And later, too, when we accompany him to his cart, Kuba does not ask anything. He embraces Father, kisses him, and says, "We'll see each other soon." But my heart tells me that we will not see him again.

59

Then the skies cleared and spring settled in. Water from melting snow filled the gullies and flooded the roads. Father rejoiced at the sight of it, and again he began to devise plans: Mother would recover, and we would take her to Czernowitz. There were good doctors in Czernowitz, doctors who stuck to medicine and didn't dabble in faith. I, too, began to recall the handsome streets and the splendid cafés in the center of town.

Twice a day we would come to the monastery, stand by Mother's bed, and gaze at her as she slept. Sometimes it seemed that she was about to wake up. This was a mistake; from day to day, her deep sleep only became deeper, and her expression never changed. The monastery doctor, a converted Jew and a monk, told Father, "Everything is in the hands of heaven. A man may decide whatever he wants, but in fact the weighty decisions are made elsewhere." Father apparently did not expect to hear such a diagnosis from a doctor and asked no further.

We were outside for most of the daylight hours, buying provisions from peasants and preparing meals next to a well or in a grove. Sometimes we would light a bonfire and roast potatoes. Roasted potatoes with butter and cheese is a delicacy. Father sipped from his flask but did not curse. He gazed at the landscape and said, "One of these days I'll come back here to paint these marvels. God has presented us with such refined forms here."

The onset of spring had apparently calmed him somewhat, and he went back to reading the works of Saint Augustine, which he had brought with him in the duffel bag. The rest of his books had been left in boxes with Victor. When Father remembered them, he'd say, "One of these days we'll need to fetch them; they're as vital to me as the air I breathe." Even his smoking had changed slightly; although he still lit one cigarette after another, he did not smoke them with the same intensity as in the winter.

In the afternoons, Father sat with the monks. Mostly he spoke and the monks listened. When Father recited long passages from the New Testament, a kind of youthful wide-eyed wonder filled their faces, as if they were hearing something that their ears were not used to hearing. Once I heard him praising the mosaics and ancient icons in the monastery. He said, "This is great art, and the time will come when students at the academy will rush here to learn from these pure-hearted artists the meaning of true yearning for God."

In the evenings we returned to the inn. The roads were bad at this time of year and had so many potholes as to be practically impassable. Few people came. Sometimes Father sat with the innkeeper, and they talked of bygone times. One evening the innkeeper said, "Years ago, many Jews lived here, and they would worship God. In this past generation, the children threw off the yoke of their religion and the yoke of their forefathers and fled to the big cities. The fathers still lived out their days here, but eventually they vanished from the world. Now there are very few Jews in the region, the synagogues are on the verge of collapse, and there is no one to repair them."

Then he told Father about the festivals and customs of the Jews in this place. On the Day of Atonement all the men would wear white clothes, and they looked like creatures from another world. "It's a pity that they've left us," he added.

"They've left because they weren't wanted," said Father.

"We loved the old Jews," said the innkeeper, a faint smile spreading across his lips.

"And the pogroms?"

"The old Jews were used to pogroms. People beat them and they accepted their suffering with love."

"You make it sound like a law of nature."

"If you like—"

"That's one crazy law!"

"Look, anyone who does not recognize the divinity of Jesus deserves to be beaten. They have to be beaten for their stubbornness."

"That's a skewed way to look at it."

"We think it's the right and just way to see it."

"It's a distortion."

"Why do you say distortion?"

"Actually, we should say that it's a *wicked* distortion." Father's anger flared up.

I was afraid of his anger and of his trembling hands. It seemed that in a moment he would get up and hit the innkeeper. "It's a wicked distortion," Father repeated angrily, and we immediately went up to our room. Father took off his clothes quickly, put on his old pajamas, and got into bed. I did not know why he had held himself in check this time. Father doesn't usually hold himself in; if he hears malicious talk or witnesses an injustice—not to mention hearing something anti-Semitic—he does not hesitate but immediately lashes out. This time he restrained himself. His restraint pained me, and I was so stirred up that I couldn't sleep for the entire night.

60

Early in the morning the bells of the monastery began to ring, and Father made me get dressed in a hurry. The path to the monastery was mired in mud. We slushed through and arrived there soaked. The monk at the entrance greeted us differently—with a deeply bowed head.

"What's happened?" asked Father.

The monk bowed even lower and did not utter a word. The other monks immediately gathered to his side and surrounded us.

"What's happened?" Father raised his head.

"Henia passed away early this morning," the monk said quietly.

"What?" said Father, his jaw dropping, as if he did not understand.

We all turned to go down the corridor and from there to the infirmary. Mother lay in the bed, propped up by a pillow, her white face suffused with an eerie calm. Father seemed to crumble all at once, and the monk grasped his forearm and held him. Suddenly the bells sprang to life again and began to toll; the sharp peals made me dizzy.

"What?" Father repeated.

"Henia is no longer suffering," whispered the monk.

In the next chamber the choir burst into song. It was a soft song and it washed over me with a kind of painful pleasantness. Father shrugged, as if refusing to accept the gift that had been offered him.

"Henia is suffering no more." Now the monk spoke out clearly.

Father grasped my hand and turned toward the corridor. The monks did not stir. We walked down the corridor into the entrance hall. The monk who had recognized Father's name bowed. Father did not thank him. We left immediately to go for a walk around the monastery.

The sun stood full and round in the sky and poured its light upon us. The ground was muddy, and it was hard to walk. Father went ahead; when he had gone some way, he noticed that I'd fallen behind and came back for me. I had become tired and asked him to stop. He did, and lit a cigarette. When we had completed the circuit, we stood at the entrance but did not go inside.

"We've arrived," said Father, as if we had carried out a mission.

We returned to the inn, and Father downed a few drinks and chatted with one of the drunks. The innkeeper, who knew everything, came up to Father and said, "God gives and God takes away."

Father didn't agree. "What's this giving and taking?" he said. "That's just haggling. If you give, you give; you don't take back. Victor, for instance, gave and did not take. He always gave."

"Which Victor are you talking about?"

"Victor from Bucharest—good, loyal Victor."

"I have no idea which Victor you're talking about," said the innkeeper, returning to his counter. Father was drunk and was now confusing scenes from the past with the present, even mentioning little Tina. Yet he wasn't angry and he didn't threaten. At noon he announced, "I'm off to sleep," and he took a long nap.

Toward evening he woke up and we returned to the monastery. Father was not drunk, but he was hazy and spoke about distant things that were apparently troubling him. In the waiting room, he took the abbot by surprise, asking him if it wouldn't be proper to give Henia a Jewish funeral, as she'd been born Jewish and had grown up in the Jewish orphanage in Czernowitz.

"But she did convert," said the abbot weakly.

"But she divorced her husband."

"But not Christianity."

"Isn't it proper to return a person's lost honor to them?"

"What honor is sir referring to?" The elderly monk smiled.

In the meantime, more monks had gathered and Father's self-confidence ebbed. "If you think otherwise," he said, "I won't interfere. Death rules us all, and it makes no distinction between Jews and non-Jews. In the end, we'll all die. And yet, it seems to me that it's preferable for a person to be gathered to his forefathers. As the Bible says, *Born a Jew and died a Jew and returned to his resting place,* even if it's an imperfect resting place," he said with a grimace.

"Henia converted. It was her wish," said the elderly monk in a soft voice.

"Correct, sir. I spoke of matters of leniency."

"Henia converted. It was a full, religious conversion. I performed it myself."

"That's right. Perhaps that's how it has to be."

"She was Christian to the depths of her soul."

"I do not doubt it, sir."

I was astounded by Father's conciliatory tone. I had

never seen him throw his arms about in such a sloppy way. And the entire time we stood there, Father was pleasant to his hosts, praised the medical care and the way we had been treated. Finally, in a voice not his own, he said, "Henia is in faithful hands," and burst into tears.

61

During the funeral Father was drunk and could hardly stand. Two monks supported him. It was a funeral without music. Father did not cry but talked loudly. The monks and the people who had gathered did not hush him, but it was clear that his confused talking disturbed them.

The wagon carrying the coffin made its way heavily. Father suddenly asked if there was still far to go, and a monk answered him as if speaking to a child, "We're already at the graveyard." The sky was blue but not open like at Halina's funeral. I stood next to Father, tired and numb.

The ceremony was conducted by one of the tall monks, who read from a book and then spoke at great length. For some reason it seemed to me that his talking prevented Mother from rising to heaven. Father apparently felt as I did. "Henia!" he burst out. "What have they done to you?" No one hushed him, and he fell silent. I did not see the lowering of the coffin and the covering of the grave.

After the funeral we returned to the monastery. Father had not yet sobered up. He turned to the monks who were supporting him as if to his brethren in suffering, telling them about his journey to Bucharest and about the anti-

Semites who had tried to ruin his exhibition. The monks paid no heed to his words, but Father went on, telling them about Victor, calling him a "ministering angel." Faint smiles flitted across their faces; then they were serious again.

During the meal after the funeral Father kept talking. He spoke of the anti-Semites who contaminate the very air we breathed. He did not speak of Mother. One of the monks said of her, "She was a noble woman, and even in sickness she conducted herself with nobility."

"And let me tell you," said Father, "it's a pity that she married that man."

"But you had in fact divorced," observed the monk.

"That is true, but we never stopped loving each other."

The monk blushed.

Then the monks went to pray. "Come, let's go out," Father said, gripping my arm, and we left immediately. The last light was still flickering in the sky as we walked along the road, and the puddles had dried up.

We left the mountain that night. At first Father wanted to go to the monastery to thank the monks, but then he decided to set off right away.

"Why leave at night?" The innkeeper tried to dissuade him.

"I still have to get to Storozynetz tonight."

"The roads are terrible—no one will want to set out at night."

"I'll pay good money."

Father drank but did not get drunk. He told me that he was thinking of taking the night train from Storozynetz to Czernowitz; immediately after that he would rent an apartment and begin to paint. "Life without painting is death." I did not envision him renting a room; instead, I saw him sitting with his friends in a tavern, drinking and cursing. I had already learned: what Father desired had very little bearing on what he did.

At midnight, before the inn closed, Father saw a wagon and stopped it. The driver hesitated at first, but eventually he agreed. Father wrapped me up in two sweaters, put a hat on my head, and we set off. As it turned out, the road had dried, and although it was a steep downward slope, the horses were careful and were able to brake the wagon when they had to.

Father buried his head in his coat. I saw again the tall monks who stood in the corridor and listened to him talk. They turned to him and said, "Why not join us? There's a large library here, and light-filled rooms where you can sit and paint. Why wander from place to place?" Father gave them a long answer with many explanations, of which I understood not a word.

The feeling that Mother was in the sky and that I was traveling to her in the wagon became much more real, perhaps because the skies suddenly cleared.

"Are you cold?" Father asked.

"No," I said, and I heard the sound of the word leaving my mouth.

Again I saw Mother as she was during the summer vacation: tall, with long, flowing hair, floating on the black waters of the lake.

62

We reached the railway station in Storozynetz sometime after midnight. It was empty, and the ticket-office windows were shuttered. Father asked the guard when the next train was leaving, and he answered indifferently, "Just five minutes ago." Two dim bulbs lit the platforms, and darkness surrounded us on all sides. We had no choice but to go to town and look for a hotel. "I was wrong," said Father, as we set off.

I remembered Storozynetz well, but in the darkness it looked different. The tall chestnut trees cast their heavy shadows on the sidewalks. We went from street to street, finally stopping at the entrance of a low house with a sign on it: HOTEL SALZBURG. Father knocked on the door. A woman opened it, and Father asked her for a bed for the night. She offered us a room with two beds.

I slept only fitfully, and again I saw the funeral. Now it seemed to me that Mother's funeral, unlike Halina's, had been hasty and short, with the monks hurrying through the prayers and dispersing rapidly.

Father awoke. "Why aren't you sleeping?" he asked.

"I can't fall asleep."

"Count to a hundred."

That old ploy, which Mother would suggest from time

to time, sounded ridiculous to me now. But I started count-ing and fell asleep.

We were late getting up. Father's request that he be woken in the morning for the six o'clock train must have been forgotten. The cleaning woman claimed that she had knocked on the door and called out that it was five o'clock and had heard Father call back, "Very good, thank you."

Father did not argue and was not angry. He ordered breakfast, and we sat and ate as if we weren't in a hurry to leave. The coffee was delicious, and Father ordered another pot. The owner of the hotel, a Jew of the old kind and involved in everything going on in the region, had of course heard of Father and immediately called his wife and daugh-ters to see the marvel. Father, initially embarrassed, even-tually responded to the owner's questions, telling him at length that he had only recently returned from Bucharest, where he had held a large exhibition, and that he was now on his way to Czernowitz. The Jew, for his part, told Father that anti-Semitism in this region was on the rise, and that now Jews were being beaten in the streets in broad daylight.

"And what do the Jews do?" Father asked.

"What can they do?"

When we reached the station it was already noon. Father went to the ticket office and asked about the times of the trains, and on the spot he decided that it was best to travel now to Campulung and rest a bit, before the vacation-ers came. I had once spent a summer vacation with Mother in Campulung, and I remembered the long boulevards and the slender poplars whose shadows trembled on the side-walks.

We left on the first train, but just as the train pulled out of Storozynetz it started to rain. At first Father was happy, but as the day went on, he grew more withdrawn, and he buried himself in his coat. We arrived in Campulung at night. It was raining heavily there, too, and we huddled near the snack counter together with the station workers. The food there did not seem fresh, and we went outside to wait for a wagon. Everything that had happened to us since we left Bucharest now seemed like one nightmare that had become entwined with another nightmare. Wagons passed us, but the drivers didn't stop. Finally a wagon stopped and we got into it.

"Take us to a hotel," called Father.

"Which one?"

"Doesn't matter."

And that's how we came to the Hotel Bukovina. The woman who owned it—a woman who was not young—welcomed us politely and immediately served us coffee and rolls. The beds were comfortable, and we slept late. In the morning we sat next to the window and ate breakfast. Suddenly I saw how past years had remained frozen here, inside the tall vases on the sideboards. Father said, "It's a hotel like those from the old days; hotels like this are vanishing."

The rains did not cease. Father's plans to take walks and show me all the wonders of the place were out of the question.

"It's a good time to sleep; sleep is no less pleasant than staying awake. A man who sleeps a week rises like new." The woman who owned the hotel spoke genially, but her voice was not pleasant. I felt that she was trying to persuade Father. He listened to her and asked some detailed questions, while she elaborated: "A week of sleep is a real adventure."

"Adventure?" wondered Father.

"Correct." The proprietress held fast to her opinion.

63

The days are gray and crawl by. Father drinks and plays poker, and the owner of the hotel has given me an old pack of cards. I read Jules Verne avidly and sketch geometric forms. Every few hours Father goes over to the window and says, "I see no end to it."

"What class are you in, Paul?" the proprietress asks me.

"I don't go to school."

"Why not?"

"I've got asthma."

"Children with asthma don't go to school?"

"I'm exempted."

"And don't you want to go to school?"

"No."

During the past two years I've been breathing naturally and haven't ever choked. And to tell the truth, even before this, my breathing didn't trouble me. My exemption from school is an achievement in which Father takes pride. "Paul doesn't go to school; I've saved him from the herd," he tells everyone. Lately it seems that Father's animosity toward school has grown. "For the sake of a little math, it's hardly worth spoiling one's entire life. To go to school is like being part of a herd; there are leaders and there are serfs. Instead of a serf-child, I have a child with a questioning heart." Now Father no longer says, "Test Paul on his math." He says, "Every day outside the school walls is freedom from prison."

Father drinks continuously, and his once handsome face is now ugly—red as a beet and blotchy. On a few occasions he has warned his gaming companions against whispering together and conspiring against him. These "companions" seem like a bunch of swindlers to me. Father loses, and I can see that his patience is running out. I'm afraid that soon he's going to jump up and hit one of them. But as it turns out, the danger comes from another quarter, in the form of a tall, blond Croatian woman who has landed here. Father, it seems, has captured her fancy, and everything he says amuses her. I've already seen women like this in Czernowitz. They laugh at everything and say, "How incredibly amusing." I am sure that Father will find her revolting, but he doesn't. He sits on the couch and tells her in great detail about his journey to Bucharest, about the exhibition, and about the anti-Semites.

"You're a Jew?" she says, wondering.

"Correct."

"You don't look Jewish."

"What's wrong with being Jewish?"

"There's nothing wrong; it's just dangerous."

Father likes the blonde's answer, and he says, "You're right about that."

"I'm always right."

Father laughs and says, "Apparently!"

Then she disappears. The days continue dark and moist, the stoves roaring day and night. Most of the time I sit in the music room, reading Jules Verne and doodling geometrical shapes. When we were near the monastery, my imagination ran free; here I can't imagine a thing. My sleep is heavy and blocked, and I don't feel connected to anyone.

One night I awake and don't see Father in his bed. I am seized with fear and want to cry out. I climb down and feel his bed—it is empty and cold. The salon and the music room are also dark. I go back to bed and wait for Father to return. Only toward morning does he come in on tiptoes and get into his bed.

I know exactly what happened.

We eat breakfast extremely late. Father's face is un-shaven and his eyes are red and puffy. He carelessly shovels hunks of bread into his mouth.

In the afternoon he plays cards and loses again. Losing makes him angry, but he neither raises his voice nor lifts his hand. Later, the blonde enters and he is irritatingly friendly when he speaks to her, complimenting her and calling her "my dear."

Every night Father disappears, and in the morning he returns on tiptoes, and each time he seems more wretched to me—the clumsy gestures of the blonde already cling to him. Sensitive to the slightest physical nuance, he has now acquired her ugly movements; he even swallows his words when he speaks. If only it would stop raining, I would drag him outside.

It's already the end of May, and there's no sign of light. After dinner, Father sits on the couch and, ticking off on his fingers, counts the cities in which he's had exhibitions. It's not his usual behavior or his usual voice. The blonde sits next to him and laughs at everything that comes out of his mouth, but the others stare at him with the look of swindlers. Now it's clear to me: they're shaking him down, and at night the blonde steals from his pockets. I've already heard him mutter: "She's been stealing again!" Father is like a caged lion, not beaten and not broken, only growling and cursing himself.

64

The days pass, and Father seems to change before my very eyes: his cheeks become sunken and an unpleasant ruddiness blooms on them. Sometimes I sense that I'm a burden, that I'm in his way, and I'd like to run away, go anyplace my legs will carry me. Father wallows in his drink, in poker games, and in keeping the blonde entertained. He is barely aware of my existence. Sometimes he'll rouse himself and say, "Paul, why don't you go to sleep?" or "Why don't you read?" I know that these are not heartfelt words; he doesn't really mean them. He's mired in the blonde's room, and it's almost three in the afternoon before he surfaces. The hotel's proprietress looks after me, serves me meals, and asks me questions. Once again, the question of school and my asthma arises.

"I'm sick with asthma and exempt from school," I repeat, time and again.

"Always?"

"Always."

The proprietress has old-fashioned manners and uses old-fashioned words. She calls me "my little sir." Sometimes we play dominos or chess. I beat her effortlessly she immediately tells her guests, but these feats make not the slightest impression on Father.

Were it not for the rain, I would run away. I already see myself working in the home of a peasant or at a Jewish grocery store. Better to work hard than to sit here and watch Father ignore me. The thought that he's entangled with the blonde and has forgotten me drives me crazy.

My dreams have returned, and again I'm with Mother, traveling with her to Vatra Dornei, or to that hidden village not far from it. I lose her for a moment at the station but then find her quickly. She is so different from the way she looked recently, and her beauty is breathtaking. I ask her about her death and her burial at the monastery graveyard. She looks at me with that full, soft gaze that I so loved, and I understand that her death was an illusion that threatened to confuse my perceptions.

"We'll always travel to Vatra Dornei," she says, and I immediately feel that I'm connected to her with my entire soul. The two of us are linked to those wonderful waters, which seem to have grown clearer during the time we weren't there, so that I can now see her movements under the water.

On awakening from the dream I'm dizzy, and it's hard for me to understand what is going on around me. The proprietress asks if I've slept well, and of course I do not tell her anything. Very gradually hotel guests emerge from their lairs and settle down at the long, set tables. They eat with gusto, gossiping and laughing, and naturally they talk about Father. Whenever they mention his name, my anger flares, and I feel like smashing the dishes on the table.

One evening the blonde comes over to me and says, "How are you, Paul?"

"Fine," I reply.

"And you aren't bored?"

"No."

It seems to me that she is about to invite me to her room. I am wrong. "The proprietress tells me that you win every game against her," she says. "Is that so?"

"Correct."

"You're very talented."

I'm angry, and I say, "Apparently."

"Like your father."

"At least."

She explodes into hearty laughter, bending over and exposing her large breasts.

Father is sitting on the sofa. My conversation with the blonde does not interest him. I see the circles of delirium around his eyes, and I know that he is drunk.

Later, before she disappears with Father, she says, "Good night, sweetie, we'll see you tomorrow morning."

I wake up early, play on the floor, or read. There is a good library here, and the proprietress allows me to look through the books. I've found a book here with Father's name in it. The author showers praises on him, calling him the "Prince of Painters in a Declining Empire." As I read that praise, Father's wretchedness grieves me all the more.

Every afternoon, when I see Father coming out of the blonde's den, I want to say, "Father, let's pack our bags and leave. Rather the rain than this disgrace. These people are cheats—even the blonde steals from you. Let's travel to Czernowitz, where we'll be among friends. The streets in Czernowitz are paved, and they aren't muddy like they are here." I want to say all this, but I don't.

"Father!" The word escapes me.

"What?"

"When are we leaving here?"

"Soon," he says distractedly.

The blonde flaunts all conventions of decency; she embraces and kisses Father in plain sight of everyone. I seethe with anger as the guests whisper and smirk. One evening, one of the guests provokes Father outright, calling him—in a contemptuous tone of voice—"Arthur Rosenfeld, the renowned painter." Father takes him to task. "You shut your mouth!" he says.

Out of sheer disdain for Father, the man says, "Why should I? Why not say it: Arthur Rosenfeld, the renowned painter, has gone to live in the provinces and settled himself in the Hotel Bukovina in Campulung."

"You shut your mouth!" Father repeats, without raising his voice. The other man apparently considers Father too drunk and woozy to touch him. He is wrong, of course. Father suddenly springs up like a lion and slugs him. Had he kept quiet, I suppose Father would have left him alone, but because he keeps goading him, Father hits him again—and hard. Chaos breaks out immediately, and a doctor is called. The blonde screams at the top of her voice, defending Father: "He is the one who provoked; he's the guilty one!"

The next day, the man who was beaten up threatens to call the police. Father does not say anything. Fortunately for us, by then the skies have cleared, and we leave the hotel without further ado.

65

Father had intended to return to Czernowitz immediately, but for some reason he did not. The rains ceased, and a huge sun hung in the sky. We wandered through villages, and at night we would lodge with a peasant or at a roadside inn. Father hardly spoke, but sometimes he would burst into tears—heartrending sobs that shook his entire body.

One evening he asked me if I would remember Mother.

"Very much so," I answered immediately.

"And you'll also remember me?"

I didn't know what to say. "Why remember? You're here with me," I replied.

The distance from village to village can be miles, and at times we found ourselves in the heart of the mountains, entirely cut off from civilization. In the hotel, my head had been full of fears; here I leaned my head on a tree trunk and fell asleep. On these endless green paths, we would chance upon peddlers, small Jewish stores, and taverns. Father spoke to the storekeepers in Yiddish. They were glad to see him and did not hide their troubles: the peasants did not pay their debts, they were attacked by wayfarers, and at night gangs would rob anyone they came across. Sometimes a storekeeper would try to keep Father from leaving, saying,

"Why not sleep with us? We have two beds made up." Once, an old Jew came up to us, placed his hands on my head, and blessed me.

The nights beneath the trees made me think of Mother, and I saw her with nothing coming between us. Father did not see anything now. His walk was a kind of thrusting forward, and I sometimes had the feeling that he was heading toward the house of that art critic who had hurt him so much, and that when he got there, he would throttle him.

One night Father muttered something about his childhood in the orphanage. When he recalled his childhood, I saw the long, chilly corridors where barefoot children would shuffle as slowly as they could, and the janitor, who stood under the light at the entrance, raising his voice, saying, "Go straight to your rooms—no hanging around!" A few years earlier Father had taken me to the orphanage and I had seen the corridors for myself. The elderly janitor had remembered Father, and they'd talked about the old days. When we left, Father had said: "He was once a strong man and we were terrified of him."

About Mother—not a word. Sometimes a groan burst forth from within him, and I knew that Father was angry with himself. When he was upset this way, he would bite his upper lip, tighten his fists, and say, "I made a mistake." One night he asked me something. I did not understand his question, and he repeated it. Eventually he said, "Not even you understand me."

A few days ago a peasant showed Father a revolver he was selling. Father checked the weapon and fired a few shots, then bought it. "Now we can sleep in peace," he said in a voice that frightened me. Sometimes I felt that the purpose of this long journey was to prepare us for our return to

Czernowitz, so Father could go back to painting. From time to time he reminisced about the weeks we had spent in Bucharest and his face was filled with longing. But the reality was different. Since Mother's death, it had been hard for me to understand what Father was talking about. Once he told me: "I'm afraid of oblivion," but he strode along like a soldier and I found it hard to keep up with him.

And so we drifted from one hill to the next. It was a green, hilly region, and at that time of the year everything was in full bloom. If a peasant threatened or cursed us, Father got angry, giving back as good as he got. And if he thought he had reason to hit someone, he hit him. He had scratches on his face and his neck, but he didn't bandage them.

"Why do you need all this?" the Jews cautioned him.

"You have to stand up to hatred."

"There are too many of them."

"That's no excuse."

All the same, the Jews liked him a lot, and whenever we were in a Jewish store the proprietress would hurry to make us a meal and the proprietor would offer us lodgings. At night, when thieves drew near the door, Father opened the window and fired. Once, he wounded one of the thieves, who fled screaming for dear life.

66

Our money was running out. It seemed as though Father had wasted most of it at the hotel. Now we were living from hand to mouth, and were it not for the storekeepers who invited us for meals and put us up, it's doubtful that we could have gone on. Sometimes they provided us not only lodgings but also tea and coffee and the kinds of dry baked goods that would keep us going for days on end.

"I made a mistake," said Father, taking a swig from his flask.

Sometimes at midday, but mainly during the evenings, we would light a bonfire, prepare coffee, and sit for hours gazing at the fire. Occasionally a word or two escaped from Father. It was hard to know if they were of blame or regret.

And so we arrived at the home of a storekeeper whom Father had called "my cousin," because he had also been orphaned in his childhood and had grown up in the orphanage in Czernowitz not that many years before Father. The Jew welcomed us and immediately went to prepare tea. His house was a small shed-like structure in the heart of the hills. The two large oaks next to it only showed how low the house was. The storekeeper had lived there for thirty years, occasionally trying to get away from that lonely place but without success. All those years, with the help of the local police, whom he bribed, he had struggled against thieves and robbers. Now the police and the robbers had made a pact, and not a night went by without intimidation or a robbery. The previous evening they had stolen his horse, and now he was completely cut off.

"Don't worry," said Father, and showed him his revolver.

"You use a gun?" The storekeeper was taken aback.

"Sometimes, when there's a need for it."

"It didn't occur to me that it's possible to buy a revolver."

"Why?"

"I don't know."

We slept at the storekeeper's house for two nights. When we were about to set out again, he asked us to stay another night. Father was reluctant to, but in the end he gave in to the man's entreaties. It was a clear summer night, full of moonlight and the scent of fresh water. We sat in the yard and drank tea. Father rallied and confided to the storekeeper that he intended to return one day and draw the surrounding landscapes.

"What do you find in them?"

"Exceptional beauty."

"I look around and see only trouble."

Father spoke about the need to uphold one's honor and protect oneself. "We have to hit back at the thugs and the anti-Semites. We must give them back as good as they give. Yes, life *is* precious, but there is something more precious — self-respect." Father talked and talked; it had been a long time since I had heard him speak with such fluency. Hearing this flow of words, the Jew looked at him and said, "You're still young; you don't know what a nest of vipers there is here."

"I do know," replied Father decisively.

"How's that?"

"From my fist; I take no pity on scum."

"I understand," the storekeeper said, and fell silent. We sat there until late, and at midnight we went to sleep.

Toward morning, before it was light, Father heard noises and opened the window. The robbers fired and Father fired back. If he hadn't jumped from the window and run after them, perhaps he wouldn't have been injured. Father gave chase, shot, and was hit. The storekeeper and his wife fell to their knees and bandaged his wound. Father was weltering in his own blood; he let out a horrible rattle and then fell silent. The storekeeper wrapped him in his coat and muttered, "You're still a child; you shouldn't see this." But I saw, and what I didn't see, my ears had heard.

A young peasant came riding up on a horse, and the storekeeper asked him to summon the Jews in the hills. The peasant rode off again, and the storekeeper shouted after him, "I'll pay you when you return." The storekeeper lifted Father up, carried him into the house, laid him on the floor, and covered him with a sheet.

I was sure this was a bad dream and that as soon as it faded Father would get up from the floor and we would be on our way. I stood where I was, and the longer I stood there, the more pressure I felt in my head.

Before long, Jews came streaming down from the hills. The storekeeper hastily told them what had happened, that Father had chased after the robbers and been shot. They immediately surrounded me so that I wouldn't see the angels of death, but I had already seen them in the form of great birds, landing on the trees in the yard.

I tried to push through to see Father, but people blocked the entrance to the room where he lay. I thought that they were hurting him. "Don't hurt him!" I shouted, and tried again to push through. Immediately everyone surrounded me.

Then they shut the door, and I didn't see what they were doing inside. The storekeeper's wife came outside and poured out buckets of water. The water flowed, then seeped into the earth. The sight of this water filled me with dread, and I ran to the blocked door. It opened and an intense prayer burst out from inside. I tried to break through the wall of people so I could see Father get to his feet, but people stopped me. "Father!" I managed to shout before falling to the floor.

67

Then they placed Father on a stretcher, and everyone set out. Wagons carrying peasants came from the opposite direction, and we moved aside so as not to bump into them. The path was green, and when we got to the hill, the sun was already sinking. Now I was sure that Father would break through and start hitting the people who were jostling him, just as he had beaten up that man who had provoked him in the hotel.

The irritating muttered prayers grew louder with every passing moment. I felt suffocated, and a shout escaped from my throat. The shout must have given me strength, for I shook myself free of the people who were clutching me, and I ran to the river. When I glanced back, I saw people running after me and surrounding me. I had run fast, and I must have gone quite some distance. The people who caught me were breathing heavily, and they dragged me back by force. The moment they eased up, I again tore myself away, but from the thicket two captors quickly emerged in ambush: two Jews in black garb.

The prayers began again. "Father! Father!" I shouted, and I spat. This must have been too much for them, because one of the Jews slapped me. The slap loosened a floodgate of tears, which ran down my face. Then they must have hidden Father from me.

On the way home, I was already bound hand and foot. People gathered around and talked to me, but I heard only my own voice: "Father! I want Father!" It was a long walk, and after a while people stopped talking to me.

Even when we returned to the house they didn't loosen my ropes. The storekeeper's wife brought me soup and coaxed me to taste it. Men stood and prayed. The muttering seeped into me. "Father! Father!" I shouted. Darkness fell and everyone dispersed; I stayed with the storekeeper and his wife. The two of them sat next to me and talked to me. I heard them, but I didn't understand a word they said. The thought that at night I could still free myself from the bonds and run away helped to stop my tears, and I fell asleep.

I slept for hours. When I woke it seemed to me that I was in the inn next to the monastery, but then I saw the bearded storekeeper and his wife, and I remembered where I was. In spite of this, I said, "I have asthma."

"What?" The mouth of the storekeeper's wife gaped open.

"I have asthma," I repeated, but I immediately understood that my words were out of place.

How long was I with them? I don't remember. They, for their part, did not loosen my bonds, and I had to stay tied to the bed, shouting and sleeping by turns.

One morning the storekeeper put me in a wagon and the three of us set out. It was summer, and the light hurt my eyes. As we drove under the tall trees I suddenly saw Father. He was tall and broad, his head inside the collar of his coat, his eyes surrounded by black circles. I wanted to shout but I couldn't. I was filled with his silence.

After a while, the storekeeper stopped next to a well to let the horses drink, and he offered me some water, too. I refused. We took to the road again, and then we were in the heart of the forest.

Toward evening we reached Czernowitz. I was astonished that people could be strolling about the quiet, shady avenues without seeing that Father and I had merged, and that now nothing could come between us. The wagon traveled down several streets. I heard the tap-tapping of Father's shoes, and I was certain that we were now going straight to the church refectory.

The storekeeper's wife started to talk to me again. I didn't answer her. Her face was pale and ugly, and it seemed to me that she was about to open her mouth and scream.

The wagon stopped outside the orphanage. The storekeeper lifted me up in his arms, and his wife knocked at the gate. The gatekeeper asked something, and the woman pointed to her husband and me. Here, too, I tried to run away, but the storekeeper was strong and grabbed my ankle and arm. The man in the office asked me my name, and I told him. When he heard it, he asked if I was the son of Arthur Rosenfeld.

The clerks who sat in the adjoining office stared at me and asked how Father was. The storekeeper told them. That was on the sixteenth of June, 1938, and I was sure that in the evening Father would come to fetch me, as he always did. The storekeeper and his wife, after they told the clerk whatever they told him, seemed pleased with what they had done, and they left.

"What would you like to eat, Paul?" asked the clerk in a very practical tone of voice.

"I don't want anything," I said without looking at him. "I'm waiting for Father."

"Your father won't be coming so quickly. You have to have patience, and in the meantime you have to eat something," said the clerk, and he went off to make a sandwich.